SERPENT'S EYE

HOSTAGE

CASE ONE:
OPERATION LYNX

STEPHEN JAMES

First published in 2009 by Miles Kelly Publishing Ltd
Bardfield Centre, Great Bardfield, Essex, CM7 4SL

Copyright © Miles Kelly Publishing Ltd 2009

10 9 8 7 6 5 4 3 2 1

Editorial Director: Belinda Gallagher
Art Director: Jo Brewer
Senior Designer: Simon Lee
Managing Editor: Rosie McGuire
Copy Editor: Vic Parker
Editorial Assistant: Ned Miles
Image Manager: Lorraine King
Production Manager: Elizabeth Brunwin
Reprographics: Stephan Davis, Jennifer Hunt

ISBN 978-1-84810-181-4

Printed in China

British Library Cataloguing-in-Publication Data
A catalogue record for this book is available
from the British Library

The author would like to thank Fabian Thomas
for his thoughtful contributions in the
preparation of this book.

Publisher's note
This is a work of fiction. Any similarities to
persons living or dead are strictly coincidental.

Author's note
Although this is a work of fiction and there is no
such organization as Serpent's Eye, the facts and
figures on drug smuggling are, to the best of my
research, correct.

Made with paper from a sustainable forest

www.mileskelly.net
info@mileskelly.net

www.factsforprojects.com
The one-stop homework helper —
pictures, facts, videos, projects and more

An overview of the structure and formation of the Serpent's Eye Executive (SEE) and Syndicate Against Terrorism and Organized Crime (SATOC)

OPERATION LYNX

REPORT A: OBJECTIVES

1. Establish location of camp where Senator Nick Finlay is held.
2. Observe and befriend Senator David Rizzo and monitor his communications.

REPORT B: OBJECTIVES

1. Amass evidence against Senator Rizzo and Estafan Peron. Establish link between them.
2. Assemble SE team and prepare for next phase.

REPORT C: OBJECTIVES

1. Locate targets and establish contact.
2. Formulate plan in situ to free targets safely and with minimum bloodshed.

REPORT D: OBJECTIVES

1. Free targets.
2. Inhibit assailants.

REPORT E: OBJECTIVES

1. Retrieve evidence.
2. Pursue suspects through all available legal channels.

John Kyle
SATOC

From a secret memo dated 3rd June, 2002
SJ

3rd June 2002

SATOC MEM JK/SE/DD12764

Re: Serpent's Eye Executive

When we decided to form SEE it was a sad moment for the world. It was an admission that the normal means of defeating threats to our society such as negotiation, diplomacy, police work and, if necessary, military force, were not adequate. It was an indication that the rift between rich countries and poor had widened. Even within the developed countries the gulf between rich and poor had grown dramatically. The old easily recognized animosities between communist and capitalist that the world had grown used to since the Second World War had virtually disappeared by the new millennium, but the climate was perfect for new adversaries to flourish.

Crime has been with us for as long as there have been laws to define it. And so has terrorism, though few can agree upon a definition of terrorism*. When terrorism joins with other types of organized crime, or extremism, or powerful new means of mass destruction, or all three, then there is a threat truly deserving of the word 'terror'.

The growing boldness of terrorist and other criminal organizations in the 21st century requires a response beyond the bluntness of a purely military one. The SEE response will be measured and minimal whenever possible. It will be based upon good intelligence and cooperation with local interests. It will use the finest recruits, selected and highly trained over a number of years in a wide range of skills. They will be hand-picked for their mental, emotional and physical qualities. We are looking for commitment and determination, not ruthlessness or savagery. We will have to select them when they are still forming ideas. Also their youth will be an essential part of their disguise.

---

* The term 'terrorism' was originally used to describe the actions of the Jacobin Club during the 'Reign of Terror' in the French Revolution. "Terror is nothing other than justice, prompt, severe, inflexible," said Jacobin leader Maximilien Robespierre.

*Colonel Davies'
profile for Operation
Lynx.*
SJ

Colonel 'Duffy' Davies, ex-SAS soldier with a keen mind and extensive knowledge of terrain, weaponry, explosives and logistics. Also an expert in the psychological pressures the Serpents will encounter. He helps train group members and then becomes their anchor man for the various missions.

Warfare, violence, crime, even terrorism, have been with us ever since as a species we could stand upright. During my years in the SAS I witnessed the ugly side of human nature, but I have also travelled the world and seen that it is a planet worth fighting for. Many of those we fight against as Serpent's Eye, do not care about the future of the world or about its inhabitants. Their aims are specific, usually self-seeking, always violent.

The 9/11 World Trade Center atrocity did not change the world, but it felt like it did at the time. It triggered many things, including the formation of SATOC and the search for you, the recruits. You are young because SATOC decided that our motivation had to come from safeguarding the future of the young, not preserving the past of the old – the world you are fighting for belongs to you. You are intelligent because your enemy is invariably cunning. You must know the latest technology – your enemy will be using it against you. You must have skills for self-defence, but also for attack when necessary. And you must both understand what you will be asked to do and believe that what you are doing is right.

When this mission is over my assistant (the admirable Susie Johns, known to all as SJ) and I will compile a file. It will include file notes, communications, briefs and debriefs, journal entries, mission status reports, recorded phone calls – everything of relevance, plus SJ's research and updates of issues connected with the mission. The file will be used as training material for future missions.

You are the first of the Serpents and this is your first mission, but it will not be the last. Sadly, the world will provide plenty of missions and will require many of you to undertake them.

Colonel Davies

Structure of SATOC/SEE operations

SATOC

SATOC is a loosely formed think tank of academics who have analyzed global security crises since the Twin Towers disaster of 2001 (9/11). It was SATOC that suggested the formation of an elite group of motivated young people who would be trained for specific actions against terrorism and organized crime. Members of SATOC pass down their analysis to the Serpent's Eye Executive (SEE) who then implement SATOC's recommendations.

Professor Stuart Amos
UK

SEE

Formed in 2002 to carry out recommendations from SATOC. SEE has identified, recruited and trained young people over a period of ten years with the first recruits 'graduating' in 2007. The SEE is headed by ex-SAS Colonel 'Duffy' Davies. SE operatives are under his command. Funding and authority for operations are not traceable to governments as many of the operations are politically sensitive. Secrecy is of the highest importance.

Recruitment

Recruitment, training and liaison are undertaken by an international board comprising ex-military and ex-secret services personnel, as well as experts in logistics and communications.

Will Sugden
Australia and Far East

Agents

Potential SE recruits were assessed by the SEE immediately after SATOC was set up. The SEE continue to look for recruits, who must be between 11 and 16 years of age, highly intelligent and physically capable.

Rik Abbot
Americas

Sleepers

'Sleepers' are made known to the SEE through government agencies such as MI6 and Interpol. Located all over the world, they are often ex-military personnel with special skills who live normal lives, but are ready to offer their services at a moment's notice.

Jules Ivory
Afghanistan

Pedro Mori
South America

Simi Nazim
UK

Technical

The Technical Division was set up to provide communications know-how, manage access to surveillance cameras including satellites, and to research and develop new technology of use to the SE operatives.

Van Dyke
Americas

John Kyle
US

Hilary Porter
Australia and Far East

Henri Destain
Continental Europe

Duncan Davies CEO
SERPENT'S EYE EXECUTIVE (SEE)

Dan Thorpe
Americas

Martin Bruggen
Continental Europe

Frank Bellini
Roaming brief

Emilia Gonzalez
Americas

Danny Smyth
UK and Middle East

Omar Mir
UK and Middle East

Eva Campbell
USA

Madi Aziz
Middle East

Ron Cheung
Far East

Natalie Cellini
Australasia

Mani Likasi
Africa

Bruno Varecci
Europe

Bulldog
UK and Europe

Marius
Australasia

Porphyry
Africa and Middle East

SEE + SATOC PROFILES

SEE global operations

World map showing the main locations of SE Operatives and sleepers. The live version is accessed via the SE website (SEWEB).
SJ

Bruno Varecci
Sleeper
Europe

BV

Jules Ivory
Sleeper
Afghanistan

Omar Mir
Agent
UK and Middle East

Danny Smyth
Agent
UK and Middle East

JI   **OM**

DS

MA

RC

Ron Cheung
Sleeper
Far East

Madi Aziz
Sleeper
Middle East

ML

NC

Mani Likasi
Sleeper
Africa

Natalie Cellini
Sleeper
Australasia

SERPENT'S EYE

SATOC

REPORT A: OBJECTIVES

1. Establish location of camp where Senator Nick Finlay is held.

2. Observe and befriend Senator David Rizzo and monitor his communications.

SERPENT'S EYE
SATOC

In compiling this file I decided it might be helpful for anyone not familiar with this mission to have an alphabetical list of people involved in Operation Lynx.
I have cheekily included myself because you might like to know who wrote the notes and provided the factual back-up.

SJ

Rik Abbot
US Serpent's Eye Operative (SEO) and team leader for Operation Lynx.

Nico Bladic
Russian Mafia soldier.

Freddy Blanco
Military trained colleague of Pedro Mori.

Eva Campbell aka 'Softshoe'
US sleeper for SEE. Also a freelance journalist for several US newspapers and magazines.

Josh Coles
Lieutenant on USS *Leviathan*, a US customs cutter. Commanded the unit that intercepted the *Esperanza*, a semi-submersible that was smuggling drugs.

Tony Cordorone
Italian Mafia boss. Rival of Viktor Timoshenko.

'Manchu'
SEE driver based in New York.

Maria Elena
FARC guerrilla befriended by Emilia Gonzalez.

Colonel Duncan Davies aka 'Duffy'
CEO of SEE. Takes instructions from SATOC and coordinates SE Operatives on missions. Called 'Briscoe' by Vince Mayhew in his magazine interviews.

Chad Derrick
Investigative journalist for VORTEX magazine known for his hard-hitting exposés.

Senator Nick Finlay
US Senator committed to revealing links between Senator David Rizzo and Colombian drugs baron Estafan Peron.

Emilia Gonzalez
US Serpent's Eye Operative (SEO) and operational second-in-command on Operation Lynx.

Susie Johns
Colonel Duncan Davies' assistant for the last seven years, based in the London office. Formerly administrator for MI5.

Eric Kim
Chinese American SEE driver based in New York.

Lev Kuznetsov
Russian Mafia. Consigliere (advisor) to Viktor Timoshenko.

John Kyle
US executive of the SATOC organization and friend of Senator Nick Finlay.

Vince Mayhew

Personal bodyguard and friend of Senator Nick Finlay.

Charles Montoya

SEE's mole in Avianca, the Colombian national airline.

Pedro Mori

SEE sleeper based in Colombia. Ex-military, ex-police. Worked with Colonel Duncan Davies in the SAS.

Diego Napa

Military trained colleague of Pedro Mori.

Jorges Ortiz

Military trained colleague of Pedro Mori.

Estafan Peron

Colombian drugs baron. Runs a legitimate business in coffee exports in parallel to his illegal activities.

Juan Pablo Picar

Henchman of Estafan Peron and highly efficient assassin.

Senator David Rizzo

On the SATOC list as someone suspected of corruption and having links with organized crime. Closely involved in the flow of US government funds into Colombia.

Enriques Rosco

Interrogator for a FARC group active in northwest Colombia.

Melanie Rose

Australian tourist abducted by FARC guerrillas along with boyfriend Tod Simmonds and SEO Emilia Gonzalez.

Eulogio Ruis

Military trained colleague of Pedro Mori.

Jhon Santiago

Military trained colleague of Pedro Mori.

Tod Simmonds

Australian tourist abducted by FARC guerrillas along with girlfriend Melanie Rose and SEO Emilia Gonzalez.

Gregory Stutz

Russian Mafia hit man.

Will Sugden

SATOC Recruitment Officer for Australia and the Far East.

Dan Thorpe

SATOC Recruitment Officer for the Americas responsible for head-hunting the SEE team on Operation Lynx.

Viktor Timoshenko

Russian Mafia boss. Rival of Tony Cordorone.

Van Dyke

Talented IT expert belonging to technical arm of SEE.

John Kyle
SATOC

12th Feb 2008

SATOC MEM JK/SE/DD59308

To Col. D Davies in strictest confidence

I am sure you know of Senator Nick Finlay – there is a detailed profile in the SATOC archives. He and I have been quietly investigating the dealings of one Senator David Rizzo who seems to enjoy wealth way beyond his income. We have been particularly interested in his connection with Colombia and the coca eradication scheme. Again, you will find everything in the archives so I won't burden you with the details.

Against my advice, Finlay went on a trip to Colombia two weeks ago to see first-hand what was happening with the scheme. His itinerary took him into territory held by FARC. Yesterday, returning from a coca farm, his escort was ambushed. We know from the Colombian sources that three of the six drivers and gunners were killed and the remainder were badly wounded. Neither Finlay nor his bodyguard, Vince Mayhew, have been found. They are either dead, or have been taken prisoner by FARC.

I think we should proceed on the assumption that Finlay has been taken by FARC. I will arrange a SATOC video conference later today and if we are all in agreement I would like you to organize the SEE team as quickly as possible.

The team will need special forces training in jungle conditions. It will take weeks, if not months, to get them up to speed. The sooner we start the better.

JK

FARC
Revolutionary Armed
Forces of Colombia

SJ

Profile on Senator Nick Finlay

Nicholas Finlay   **DOB** 15.01.1960

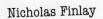

Family Parents: Joseph Patrick Finlay and Debra Horton

Education University of Memphis, TN, Law School

Career Born in California. His father was a factory worker and his mother taught fourth grade. His older sister, Stacey, died from a drugs overdose while Finlay was in his last year at college.

His parents had liberal values, which no doubt influenced Finlay's eventual choice of career – as a democrat nominee in 1986 during the Reagan presidency. In 1996, a time when the US had a Democratic president in Bill Clinton, Finlay joined the House of Representatives and became a Senator in 2000. He served on numerous committees, but took a special interest in South America. He challenged the Plan Colombia initiative and in doing so clashed heads on several occasions with Senator David Rizzo. Finlay is a friend from college days of SATOC's John Kyle.

Locations Spends much of his time in Washington DC where he owns an apartment. Also rents an apartment in Bogotá.

Interests Active on several charities, one of which supports victims of drug crime.

SERPENT'S EYE
SATOC

David Rizzo on his yacht

Profile on David Rizzo

David Anthony Rizzo

DOB 24.11.1967

Family Parents: Anthony Rizzo (second-generation Italian), Maureen Dickens

Education St Johns Hopkins University, NY, Business Studies

Career Born in Idaho and grew up on a ranch. Graduated from Johns Hopkins University in 1988 before working for Merchant Alliance Inc, a private bank in Manhattan. In 1995 he visited Bogotá, Colombia, to help set up a Colombian office for the bank. It was on this visit that he met with Estafan Peron and began a money laundering operation through the new Bogotá office. However Rizzo craved power in addition to wealth and, using his money to fund a campaign, he ran for office in 2004. He was on several committees including one working on a controversial proposal to give US gun manufacturers broad protection from civil lawsuits. Vague allusions were made in the press regarding some of his friends, among whom are New York Mafia bosses. He is believed to have misappropriated funds from a coca eradication scheme funded by the US government, and made sizeable loans to his Mafia connections.

Locations A hunting lodge with 500 acres near Craig, Colorado; an apartment in Washington; an apartment in Manhattan; a summer house on Martha's Vineyard where he moors a yacht and a speedboat. His property portfolio was estimated at $37.2m in 2007. Now valued at $25.6m.

Category Probably not physically dangerous – prefers to kill elk at a distance, rather than people close up.

Weaknesses An intemperate nature, craves money and power, a lecher.

Rizzo's yacht 'The Huntress'. Estimated value $6.5m

The hunting lodge in Colorado. Estimated value: $3.8m

Peron's New York apartment.
Estimated value: $3.5m

Peron's yacht 'Constanza'.
Estimated value: $55m

A rare photo of Peron.
He is on his ranch
near Zaragoza.
Estimated value: $30m

Profile on Estafan Peron

Estafan Julio Peron

DOB 02.05.1956

Family Parents: Victor Patino Peron and Silvia Catalina Fomanques
Wife: Constanza Meruz (married in 1988) Children: Cesar, Javier and Natalia

Education Universidad de Santander, Bucaramanga, Degree in Chemical Engineering

Career Parents were landowners in North West Colombia. Both were murdered while Peron was still at university by person or persons unknown. Peron inherited 700 hectares of farmland (mostly banana plantations), which he then systematically turned to coca production. His farms have a reputation for pollution, low wages and intimidation of farm workers. He has kept himself immaculately clean when it comes to cocaine production by buying off law enforcement agencies and even the judiciary. In 1995 he met Senator David Rizzo and the two have since collaborated in drug wholesaling, money laundering, fraud and corruption. Evidence of these activities has been impossible to find, though John Kyle of SATOC is certain of the facts. Kyle is a friend of Senator Nick Finlay, who has instigated a secret investigation into the activities of Peron and Rizzo.

Locations A fortified hacienda near Caucasia, North West Colombia; a ranch near Zaragoza; a luxury apartment in Bogotá; a luxury villa outside Cartagena where he moors his $55m yacht; a penthouse overlooking Central Park, NY. Estimated property worth $230m.

Category Ruthless, but careful to distance himself from the evil he trades in. Issues cold-blooded commands to his lieutenants.

Weaknesses Thinks himself beyond the law and beyond retribution.

A good man in Colombia

Senator Nick Finlay wanted to meet with coca farmers and discuss with them why Plan Colombia was not working. What happened next is a story of deadly intrigue in the jungle.

By Chad Derrick

Senator Nick Finlay was not someone you would expect to see in the jungles of northern Colombia. This avuncular man in his late forties with iron-grey hair and penetrating eyes, snappily dressed in his Liana Lee suits, looked more at home at Signatures restaurant in DC than boarding a Huey gunship dressed in military fatigues (the latest photo we have of him). The Huey took him to the jungle town of Barrancabermeja where he was met by a military escort consisting of a solitary Humvee and two battered Land Cruisers. Each vehicle had a driver and an armed soldier of the Colombian army. Finlay was accompanied by his aide and bodyguard Vince Mayhew. They were about to enter fiercely contested FARC territory and Mayhew was not happy with the level of protection.

ABOVE: Senator Nick Finlay being interviewed in front of the Capitol building in January 2008.

The destination was a 'cocina' – a jungle cocaine kitchen or processing plant – near Zaragoza. Finlay wanted the first-hand experience of meeting with the coca farmers and discussing with them why Plan Colombia was not working. Where was that $1.6 billion of US money going? Were the farmers receiving the Plan's compensation monies in return for them destroying their coca bushes? Why was cocaine production up instead of down? Why was Colombian cocaine still being sold openly on the streets of Chicago, Los Angeles and Manchester? Why were young lives still being devastated by the sale of crack cocaine in Rome and Marseilles and just about every other city in the developed world?

I arranged to meet Mayhew for this interview in an isolated farmhouse in Nebraska. He was concerned about the secrecy of our location and instructed me in precautions I should take to ensure that I wasn't followed. Upon my arrival he went through my briefcase with a professional thoroughness before he was prepared to start the interview.

Derrick: Take me from the trip into the jungle by helicopter.

Mayhew: The Huey carried its usual crew of four, including two gunners, plus myself and Finlay. We were flying low over the jungle canopy to give the trigger-happy FARC shooters no time to take a pop. But for a few minutes we flew along the path of a river, which seemed like poor tactics to me. Sure enough, I saw some flashes of automatic fire from a hide near the river bank and the Huey was hit near the tail. The pilot took violent evasive action and dived for cover back over the jungle.

That could have been it, there and then. It told me that the security of the mission was compromised and that the team we were with were at best inexperienced, at worst dangerously stupid. I told Finlay we should abort, but he'd have none of it.

"No one said this would be a walk in the woods Vince."

"Sure," I said. "You're the boss." But by this point I was seriously worried.

We landed in a clearing at

ABOVE: The Huey leaves after delivering Finlay and Mayhew to the jungle rendezvous.
BELOW: From Barrancabermeja, Finlay and Mayhew travelled to an area near Zaragoza by road.

Mayhew agreed to be interviewed by Derrick on the understanding that real identities would not be used. Vortex's publishers failed to comply with this request, as you will see on the following pages. We were unable to prevent publication, and as a result we have had to change the identities of some operatives and retire others completely.

SJ

10.20 hours to rendezvous with the convoy. FARC and the government had established a DMZ where we were heading, so that meant no helicopters and no soldiers and in theory at least, no FARC. Our escort was to be some trusted paramilitaries – all of them vetted by our embassy security guys in Bogotá. We felt comfortable with that. The escort was a Humvee with two crew, and two beaten up Land Cruisers with two tough-guys apiece. It looked okay for a walk in the woods, but not these woods.

We got started at 10.45 hours driving on jungle logging roads. We were in the Humvee with a Land Cruiser behind and one in front. We drove for an hour and 20 minutes to get to the cocina. It was just a small clearing with a few huts for stores and chemicals and the so-called kitchen where they made their evil stuff. Finlay was shown round the place by some poor-looking guys in rags who looked as though they needed a decent meal. Finlay did what he's good at – he listened and when he spoke he did so in his perfect Spanish. The farmer guys were clearly impressed and they gave him what he wanted – the truth. Seems these guys had tried grubbing up bushes and going clean. They were told they'd get some compensation just like it says in the good ol' Plan Colombia. They got compensation alright. The coffee bushes they'd planted were torched with a flame thrower and two of them were garrotted. They were told to get back to the coca business right away or they would all feel the piano wire on their throats.

These are farmers, not fighters. They can scrape a living from making cocaine or they can be killed if they don't. When we left the cocina Finlay was about to

Coffee farmers turned cocaine producers – these are some of the cocina workers that Finlay met and spoke to.

This gives some good background on cocaine

SJ

COCAINE

Chemical name:
Benzoylmethyl Ecognine

Definition:
Cocaine is the alkaloid found in the leaves of the coca plant, *Erythroxylon coca*. It is a central nervous system stimulant. For thousands of years, coca leaves have been chewed by the inhabitants of the Andean regions of South America to combat the effects of apoxia (altitude sickness), increase energy and depress appetite. Since the late nineteenth century, cocaine has also been used in licensed drugs such as a local anaesthetic in certain kinds of surgery and in medicines for particular eye and ear problems. However, cocaine is also highly addictive and since the 1960s has had a widespread history of recreational abuse across the globe.

Description:
In its purest form, a white crystalline powder.

Mode of action:
Cocaine acts upon the central nervous system, affecting a part of the brain called the *ventral tegmental area*, and in turn the connecting *nucleus accumbens*, which is a 'pleasure centre'. It also blocks the reuptake of the neurotransmitter dopamine, which builds up in the nervous system. These actions cause immensely pleasurable feelings of euphoria and of having elevated physical and mental powers.

Mode of administration:
Cocaine loses potency when taken by mouth, so recreational drug users either snort it or dissolve it in water and inject it. Crack is a smokable form of cocaine. Both cocaine and crack may be used with other substances, such as smoking with marijuana and injecting with heroin.

Effects of use:
The grandiose excitement created by cocaine is short-lived, only 5 to 15 minutes, and as the drug wears off, a corresponding deep depression is felt. This motivates recreational drug users to take another dose, to restore the positive feelings. In this way, users become addicted for psychological reasons to the drug. (Habitual users have been known to inject small doses every ten minutes – totalling as much as 10 grams in one day.)

Side-effects can include: chronic runny nose; increased energy causing restlessness; decreased appetite causing weight loss and disorders due to malnutrition; irritability, mood swings and paranoia; rapid heartbeat, chest pains and heart attacks; respiratory failure; auditory and visual hallucinations; strokes; convulsions; death due to overdose.

Testing:
A urine test can detect cocaine use.

Street names:
Coke, blow, Charlie, flake, snow, toot.

Cocaine being made in a cocina (left) plus a SATOC file photo on drug abuse.

SJ

Finlay and Mayhew threw themselves out of a Colombian Army Humvee like this one.

explode. He was angry that it took a visit from him to confirm that there was a big problem, when they had people on the ground in the area. He even mentioned the possibility of what he called a 'snake' in the senate. I think he knew the name of the snake he had in mind, but he wasn't about to tell me.

It was 16.10 hours when we set off back to the chopper landing site. The chopper was due at 17.00 hours so we had to get a move on. The lead Land Cruiser decided on a short-cut that would take us over a bridge. When we arrived at this bridge I was horrified – it was a rickety wooden bridge about 50 yards in length that was made for a donkey and cart and not a three-tonne Humvee. The river was fast and brown and ugly. We had to take the bridge one vehicle at a time and slowly, very slowly.

The lead Cruiser made it okay and waited for us on the other side. It was when we were half-way across that both Cruisers were hit with grenades and automatic fire at close range. The guys in the vehicles didn't stand a chance – it was plain and simple bloody murder.

That left us stranded in the middle with shooters on both sides of us. A voice from a megaphone said, in Spanish, "Drive forward or we will blow the bridge up. Please don't make me repeat this." Our driver and his side-kick were clearly terrified and just looked back at Nick and I helplessly.

I had to make a quick decision, or we'd have been in the hands of FARC in a few seconds. I said to Finlay, "We have to jump, Nick – it's our only chance." He gave me a quick nod and with that I threw open the door and we both jumped into the rushing waters. I heard a burst of machine gun fire and then nothing but the sound of the water and my own

breathing and gasping. Despite us being strong swimmers, the strength of the water was too great. If it hadn't been for the fishing net I think we might well have drowned.

Derrick: Tell me about the fishing net.

Mayhew: The net was strung across the river to catch bagre and picua fish – both good eating. Instead, we ended up in the net and managed to pull ourselves to the bank, half drowned and exhausted. I guess we'd gone about a mile downstream – not far enough. The FARC caught up with us before we'd gone a hundred yards into the jungle and you know the rest.

The 'rest' was that Mayhew was dumped in a backstreet in Barrancabermeja, thrown back to the Colombian authorities like an undersized fish. Finlay was the most valuable hostage FARC had bagged in years.

Part two of this interview will appear in the March edition of *VORTEX*.

REPORT A · REPORT B · REPORT C · REPORT D · REPORT E

The M998 High Mobility Multipurpose Wheeled Vehicle (HMMWV or Humvee)

SATOC INFOBASE
FILE: 302B

The Humvee's engine air intake, exhaust, electrical wires and similar parts are designed so that the vehicle can drive through water more than one metre deep. Humvees are so tough they can be dropped by parachute from cargo planes.

Cupola fitted with a powerful machine gun

Plates cover most of the bodywork to protect against bullets, land mines and other dangers

High exhaust

6.5 litre diesel engine with fuel injection

The main frame has two long girder-like rails and several cross-members

I found this in the Infobase. Thought it might be of interest to some of you petrol-heads!

SJ

SERPENT'S EYE SATOC

Message from Colonel Davies passed by hand to Eva Campbell, aka 'Softshoe'. SJ

Col. D. Davies
DD/EC25208
03.06.08

We have reason to believe that Senator Rizzo is involved in some less than totally honest accounting of funds for coca eradication schemes in Colombia. We need evidence and we need it fast. Rizzo is very cautious. You will need to use every means available to entrap him. I have asked Natasha Schmidt, one of John Kyle's arty friends, to get you an introduction to him. More instructions and contacts will follow soon – same method.

Schmidt is an art buyer in New York. She is well connected with the city's rich and powerful. SJ

Report on Rizzo

I really don't approve of this! SJ

11th June: Over a week of research and digging and I can find few chinks in Senator Rizzo's armour. I now know some of his likes and dislikes though. He adores fine dining, he hunts deer and enjoys his lodge in Colorado every summer, not surprisingly he is a strong defender of the right to bear arms, he drives a big SUV specially kitted for hunting, he is passionate about NASCAR and, this is really unexpected – collecting the works of Frederic Remington. He also has a weakness for pretty brunettes – now isn't that fortunate.

19th June: Tracking this man is really quite difficult. His office must spend a fortune on air tickets – all first class of course. But at least he keeps a regular schedule. He is on several sub-committees, apart from his involvement

with Funds for Colombia. Apparently his response to the news that Finlay is being held by FARC was supremely callous. Essentially: 'Serves the ▨▨▨▨▨ right. He had no business being there in the first place.'

23rd June: A stroke of luck. There is a Remington exhibition at Ogdensburg starting next week and Rizzo is naturally attending and so is Remington expert and NASCAR enthusiast Eva Campbell!

2nd July: The Remingtons were brilliant (sample attached) and our man Rizzo is a prize creep! When the lovely Natasha introduced me as his perfect companion for the evening, I am sure I saw him lick his lips. Lucky for SE that I love my job. I've noticed, I won't tell you how, that he has two cell phones.

Softshoe's SE Journal

One is a regular Blackberry that he uses all the time for Senate business and the other is a Nokia. I saw him use this just once and then he put it in his bag as though he wouldn't be needing it again. The next time I saw him use the second phone it was a Nokia still but a different model. I think this is his secure phone – one he then disposes of.

7th July: Oh joy (not)! Rizzo just called (from his Blackberry I noticed) to invite me to a NASCAR event at Daytona Beach. All I know about NASCAR is that it's very loud, and incredibly boring. I have attached some info for Duffy because he'll probably love it. I've asked Van Dyke to make up the tiny gadget Duffy sent me. Our technical expert is designing the device as a NASCAR pin for Rizzo's jacket. Rizzo speaks and my cell phone is dialled and automatically records. Neat. Just as long as he actually wears the pin.

REMINGTON: All American Vision

Frederic Remington Art Museum

1st July–2nd October 2008

Softshoe made contact with Rizzo at the Remington show

Frederic Sackrider Remington was an American painter, illustrator, sculptor and writer whose work centred on the lives of cowboys, Native Americans and the US Cavalry in the American West during the late 19th century. He had a huge influence on public perception of the 'wild west'.

Remington was born in Canton in northern New York on 4 October 1861. His love for all things to do with horses, the outdoors and the military stemmed from childhood, as Remington's family had a tradition of being fine horsemen – in fact, his father had been a cavalry officer in the Civil War. When Remington wasn't riding, hunting, swimming and camping he liked nothing better than to make sketches of cowboys, soldiers and horses in outdoor scenes instead. Remington's father sent him to two military schools, but Remington never showed the makings of a soldier, nor did he do particularly well academically. He began studying Art at Yale University, though he found that he felt restricted by formal art training and practising still life studies, and much preferred the imaginative freedom of action drawing. Remington's first published piece of work was a cartoon of a 'bandaged football player' for the student newspaper Yale Courant. (He was himself a member of the Yale football team.)

In 1879 Remington left Yale after only a year and a half to be with his father, who was suffering from tuberculosis. After his father's death a year later, Remington realized the dreams he had had since childhood. He travelled to Montana in 1881, at the age of nineteen, to see the 'wild west' for himself – enormous prairies, wild herds of buffalo and cattle, and the last important battles between Native American tribes and the US Cavalry. During this time Remington lived largely off his inheritance – though he did sell his first piece of artwork: a sketch published by Harper's Weekly. In 1883, Remington moved to Kansas, where he tried sheep ranching for a year before giving up this tough life and moving back home. He returned to Kansas in 1884 having married his long-standing girlfriend Eva Caten. Remington invested money in a saloon there, but as this made little income, he renewed his efforts with sketching and painting and began to make income from selling his work.

Logged in as SJ

I did a bit of research into NASCAR on SEWEB. SJ

NASCAR

NASCAR is an official body which oversees many types of motor racing around America. It was founded by Bill France Sr on 21 February 1948, and the acronym stands for the National Association for Stock Car Auto Racing. The association's headquarters are in Daytona Beach, Florida. The three top series NASCAR is in charge of are: the Sprint Cup Series, the Nationwide Series and the Craftsman Truck Series.

When most people talk about NASCAR racing they are referring to the NASCAR Sprint Cup Series. A NASCAR Sprint Cup racing car is based on a four-door American-made car, such as a Ford Fusion or a Dodge Charger. However the vehicles are specially customised with souped-up monster-power engines and extra bodywork to withstand tough side-to-side contact between cars. The NASCAR Sprint Cup series consists of 36 races on 22 different tracks which vary in size from the huge 4.28-km Talladega Superspeedway down to the 0.84-km Martinsville Speedway. Each race is a brightly-coloured whirl of noise, excitement, danger and dust.

The National Association for Stock Car Auto Racing

SERPENT'S EYE
SATOC

File note from Col. Davies

The colombian national airline

Our sleeper inside Avianca, Charles Montoya, has made contact with the FARC interrogator Enriques Rosco. Montoya has gained Rosco's trust by feeding him (low-grade) information about the comings and goings of various dignitaries through Avianca. In the photo of Finlay that FARC released last week, Rosco was in shot. It seems that his FARC group is the one holding Finlay.

Montoya has 'leaked' to Rosco that a Mr Abbot and a Miss Gonzalez will be holidaying in South America soon, and that Miss Gonzalez's family is extremely wealthy. We will bait our trap with Gonzalez. Rosco's group will abduct her and take her to the camp where Finlay is held. Gonzalez's transmitting device will enable a team, led by Abbot, to locate the camp and free Gonzalez and Finlay.

SE Operatives Field Journal

SE Operatives are encouraged to keep a daily log of events when circumstances allow. Electronic communications are fine when they work, but pen and paper never fail. The SE log is unlike any other – the 'diary' has a combination lock which, if forced, ruptures a capsule of dye. This instantly soaks the entire log (and very probably the uninvited reader) with a permanent green wash, rendering the journal entries illegible.

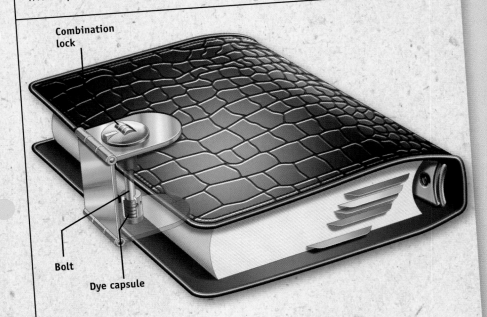

Combination
lock

Bolt

Dye capsule

File added: 21.08.2008
SE/DD25508

SERPENT'S EYE
SATOC

Rizzo and Peron keep one-off cheap pay-as-you-go cell phones for emergency calls. Once the call has been made the phones are destroyed.

Phone intercept: 20.08.08, 15:32

Rizzo: Why are you using the phone? We agreed no phone calls.

Peron: Your line is secure and so is mine – relax. After this call you'll destroy your phone just as I will. No one will know.

Rizzo: Let's make it brief then.

Peron: I am very concerned about your colleague – the one who is on a long vacation at the moment. He may be indiscreet about certain information that could be embarrassing to us both. You know who I refer to?

He is referring to Finlay and the fact that Finlay is onto the corruption and embezzling of the Colombian funds

Rizzo: Sure, but he is not likely to be returning to work.

Peron: Stranger things have happened – even quite recently.

Rizzo: That was pure luck.

Ref to Betancourt's rescue by Colombian Army from a FARC camp

Peron: It would be bad luck for us.

Rizzo: What did you have in mind?

Peron: I have some contacts near to where your colleague is taking his vacation. They could find out where he is staying and (speak) with him.

'Speak' is code for kill

Rizzo: I understood that no one knew exactly where he was staying. And our mole in FARC is...

conversation was lost at this point because of noise of traffic

Peron: ...but with a little persuasion – find the exact location.

Rizzo: This must not go wrong. You know that, don't you?

Peron: It could go wrong if we don't act soon. I don't like... uncertainty.

Rizzo: Alright then. Let's do it.

Peron hangs up

Photo, taken by Gonzalez, of Abbot soon after their arrival in Quito.

SJ

Journal of Rik Abbot –
Operation Lynx Team Leader

<u>10 Sept:</u> The flight from New York was cramped as hell – just when are they going to get around to designing a plane for someone over six feet in height? I listened to my iPod to take my mind off the lack of legroom and let the latest Isis download work its magic. Em was fine, she's only 5'3" – practically pocket-sized. She can handle herself though, believe me. She's super-intelligent, funny, and, just for the record, drop-dead gorgeous as well. She gets her music fix listening to minimalists like Philip Glass and Steve Reich. At first I just didn't get it, but she's winning me round.

First day in Quito

First impression on arriving at Quito was that there'd been an explosion in a paint store. The colours are amazing — the Ecuadorian clothes and market stalls are just alive with bold primary colours. We bought the obligatory knitted hats. Em's makes her look charming and pretty and mine makes me look like a total geek.

Found an OK hotel near the bus station called Los Alpes. Collected the ingredients from the pharmacy for the concoction that is supposed to give me all the signs of a terrible illness and a reason for Em to venture off without me and become bait for the trap. Can't say I'm looking forward to any of that. I had the distinct impression we were followed to the hotel by a girl in a blue anorak. She could have been a thief looking for some tired and dopey travellers, but she didn't act like your run-of-the-mill pick-pocket. We aim to get a pizza, a beer and some good zzzs in tonight as the bus leaves at 7am for Mindo. I know this is serious business, but I have to say I am really enjoying this part at least.

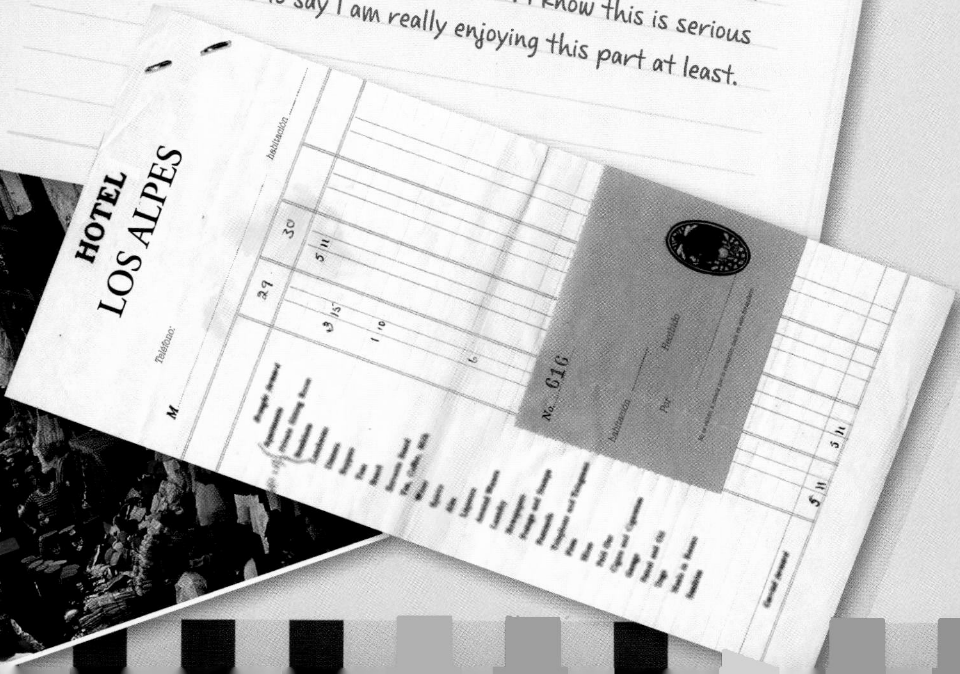

HOTEL
LOS ALPES

No. 616

Sept 11: The two-hour bus ride was incredible. We went through a small village on the equator. Stopped on the line itself and took the usual cheesy photos. The road was crazy, narrow and with sheer drops, and the drivers all seemed to share a death wish (including our bus driver). See photo attached. We gained a new shadow on the bus — a short guy in his thirties in standard issue poncho and woollen hat. Finally (several pints of sweat lighter) we arrived at Mindo, where we sampled the hotels. In one there was an amazing bug as long as my hand with bright, yellow, almost intelligent eyes. I haven't identified it yet. Tomorrow we take the bus across the border into Colombia and then stop at Ipiales.

Ecuador

Whether you're a nature lover, an adrenaline junkie, a culture vulture or a pleasure seeker, you'll find your heart's content on a trip to Ecuador. Although it is the second smallest country in South America, it arguably has the most to offer.

Wherever you are in Ecuador, the scenery is spectacular. The towering peaks of the Andes run down the central spine of the country, forming the fertile plateau of the sierra. Away to the east spreads the sparsely populated dense tropical rainforest of the Oriente and upper Amazon basin. While to the west lies the sultry mangrove swamps and sandy bays of the Pacific coastline. As Ecuador is no bigger than the state of Nevada, it's perfectly possible to breakfast by the beach, lunch amid glaciated mountains, and have supper in lush jungle, all in the same day. Ecuador is renowned for its biodiversity — named by Conservation International as one of just seventeen 'megadiverse' countries, it has 1600 species of bird (15% of the world's known bird species), 6000 species of butterfly and over 3500 species of orchid. Take a sea kayak trip into the untamed depths of the Amazon and you'll meet monkeys, toucans and tapir. You may even spot the elusive jaguar. Venture as far as the famed Galapagos Islands, nearly 1000 km

Traveller's Guide to South America

Some background information used by Abbot and Gonzalez on their travels. SJ

Ceticia anaconda

Capybara

Giant bird spider

west of the mainland, and you'll be stunned by species of plants, reptiles, birds and marine life that are not found anywhere else on the planet.

If you're after thrills rather than wildlife, bike down the side of Pichincha Volcano, hike in the endangered Bellavista Cloudforest, or go whitewater rafting through the Western Andes. To relax, rest your aching muscles in the hot springs at Papallacta. Then savour the rich heritage of Ecuador's fourteen million people by taking a trip to the Inca ruins of Ingapirca. Or stroll around the Otavalo street market and admire the locals' stunning traditional costumes and skilled handicrafts and artefacts for sale. You must not miss the beautifully preserved colonial architecture of the historic old towns of Quito and Cuenca, both named UNESCO World Heritage sites. And finally, for a thoroughly modern Ecuador experience, sample the nightlife in the buzzing bars and clubs of Baños.

Nowhere else in Latin America can you find such a diversity of activities, cultures, landscapes and climates in such a compact, accessible area.

Ecua

34

Western South Am
bordering the Paci
the Equator, betwe
and Peru

total: 283,560 sq k
land: 276,840 sq k
water: 6720 sq km
note: includes Gala

Area – comparativ
slightly smaller tha

Land boundaries:
total: 2010 km
border countries: C
590 km, Peru 142
Coastline: 2237 k

Maritime claims:
territorial sea: 200
continental shelf:
2500-m isobath

Climate:
tropical along coas
cooler inland at hi
tropical in Amazo
lowlands

Terrain:
coastal plain (cost
Andean central hi
and flat to rolling
(oriente)

Elevation extrem
lowest point: Paci
highest point: Ch

Natural resource
petroleum, fish, t
hydropower

Land use:
arable land: 5.71
permanent crops
other: 89.48% (2

Irrigated land:
8650 sq km (200

CARACAS

cia

ENEZUE

San Fernando
de Apure

BRAZ

42

REPUBLIC OF COLOMBIA /
REPÚBLICA DE COLOMBIA

Northern South America, bordering the Caribbean Sea between Panama and Venezuela, and bordering the North Pacific Ocean, between Ecuador and Panama.

Geographic coordinates:
4 00 N, 72 00 W

Area:
1,141,748 square km (includes the San Andrés y Providencia archipelago). With an area more than twice that of France, or almost three times the size of the US State of Montana, Colombia is the fourth largest nation in South America (after Brazil, Argentina and Peru). It is the 26th largest nation in the world.

Terrain:
Columbia is dominated by three branches of the high Andes Mountains – the Cordillera Occidental, running adjacent to the Pacific coast, the Cordillera Central, running between the Cauca and Magdalena River valleys, and the Cordillera Oriental, stretching north east to the Guajira Peninsula. Lowland plains stretch along the Caribbean coast and Pacific coast, ranging from the savanna of the Orinoco River basin, to the jungle of the Amazon rainforest.

Climate:
Tropical, but cooler with altitude.

Population:
39,500,000 approx. This is the second largest population in South America, after Brazil, and the 29th largest population in the world. 34.5 people per sq km. 73% urban, 27% rural – main urban centres located in the highlands of the Andes mountains. The majority of Colombians are of mixed European and Amerindian ancestry. Pure indigenous Amerindians comprise only 1% of the population.

Official language:
Spanish. Colombia has the third largest Spanish-speaking population in the world after Mexico and Spain. However, over 80 languages are spoken, many indigenous.

Religion:
95.4% Roman Catholic

Capital city:
Bogotá, population approx 6,750,000 – at 2600 m up in the Andes, it is the highest city of its size in the world.

Government:
The Constitution of 1991 established the government of Colombia as a presidential representative democratic republic. The President is both head of state and head of government, followed by the Vice President and the Council of Ministers. At provincial level are department governors.

Main agricultural products:
Crops – sugarcane, potatoes, plantains, rice, bananas, cassavas, corn, coffee, flowers. Livestock – cattle, sheep, pigs, chickens.

Main mined products:
petroleum, natural gas, gold, coal, iron ore, nickel, copper, emeralds.

Main manufactured products:
foods, textiles, chemicals, machinery, electrical apparatus, transport equipment, metal products.

Main exports:
coffee, petroleum and petroleum products, fruits, flowers, iron and steel, textile and apparel.

Main imports:
machinery, chemicals, transport equipment.

Unit of currency:
Peso.

Ecology:
Colombia is one of the world's 17 'megadiverse' countries.

Environmental issues:
Deforestation. Soil and water quality damage from overuse of pesticides. Air pollution, especially in Bogotá, from vehicle emissions. As part of the Pacific Ring of Fire, Colombia is also subject to volcanic eruptions and occasional earthquakes.

12 Sept: Once in Colombia we went to Ipiales, a pretty crappy border town. It was very different from Ecuador, more westernized. We changed our dollars to pesos, and there are about 2000 pesos to the dollar, meaning we were spending thousands — our bus journey was 1600 pesos! We stayed in a very basic hotel in Ipiales. My bed was a piece of foam rubber and a sheet and smelled of vomit. We were both bitten by bed bugs and have the lumps and blotches to prove it. Need to find a slightly healthier hotel before taking the 'compound'. I realize time is of the essence so I'll take the evil stuff tonight. It's comforting to know that Em has had some medical training.

Em thinks she caught sight of poncho man dressed in jeans and T-shirt. There is a juice bar across the road and she saw him drinking there. She snapped a photo of him using her iPhone.

REPUBLI
COLOM
MINISTERIO DE RELACIO

Clase / Categoria / Type / Category

Apellidos / Surname
RIK ABBOT
HOLAN...

Bed bug on Em's leg!

Departures / Sorties
27.05.01 25
AMSTERDAM SCHIPHOL
C 027

JAMAICA ON CONDITION THAT THE
...ONGER THAN...
... ANY FORM OF EMPLOYMENT IN THE
...CCEPT ANY ORDER FOR GOODS OR
...HALF OF ANY PERSON, FIRM OR
...ON BUSINESS WITHIN THE ISLAND.
...FFIC R
1001

Poncho man

SERPENT'S EYE
SATOC

search

Go | Search

navigation
- Main page
- Contents

toolbox
- What links here
- Related changes
- Upload file
- Special pages
- Printable version
- Permanent link

languages
- العربية
- Беларуская (тарашкевіца)
- Català
- Česky
- Dansk
- Deutsch
- Español
- Esperanto
- Euskara
- فارسی

Inflation in Latin America

Inflation is perhaps the biggest challenge for Latin America today. The factors which have caused this are specific to each country, but in general they include: fast-growing economies where the demand for commodities such as food and clothing outstrips supply, causing a reliance on more expensive foreign imports and skyrocketing prices; spiralling oil costs (causing increased prices for water, electricity and gas); plus government controls on minimum wages and price indexes. The large number of United States dollars that enter Latin America illegally because of the drugs trade also contributes to inflation – as does the decline in local food production because large areas of land are devoted to producing drug crops instead of agriculture. Double-digit inflation (estimated by some economists to be as high as 25% in Argentina) has resulted in the impoverishment of the middle class throughout Latin American countries – when people go out to buy goods they spend more and return with less. Inflation has also adversely affected tourism – why would a traveller want to go somewhere that is more expensive than comparable locations? Solutions are complex and constantly debated among economists.

Poverty in Colombia

A displaced woman washing laundry in a refugee community in Cali.
Photo: Colombia Journal

14 Sept: Well that evil brew was effective alright! By the morning of yesterday my temperature had soared to 103 degrees and I was jabbering like a monkey. Em made sure that the hotel staff knew that I was in a bad way and called the local doctor. He advised (as we knew he would) getting to Bogotá where I'd get better treatment. Em told him that she knew what medicines I needed because this had happened to me before and that she would have to go to Bogotá herself and come back with the drugs. She left first thing to get the bus. I still feel terrible, but don't want to die any more, unlike a few hours ago. The vertigo has eased off. My temperature, according to Em's thermometer, is just over the 100 mark and I am not going to the bathroom every ten minutes. Progress then! Must get some sleep.

New Message | Cancel

To: R

AYV? F stpn bus. NT4M <3 M

Send

Text message from Gonzalez to Abbot: Are you vertical? FARC stopping bus. No time for more (heart shape) Em

SJ

SERPENT'S EYE

SATOC

SEE TOP SECRET

REPORT B: OBJECTIVES

1. Amass evidence against Senator David Rizzo and Estafan Peron. Establish link between them.

2. Assemble SE team and prepare for next phase.

Evening *Times* | 20th September 2008

Three tourists taken hostage

A few weeks after there were celebrations over the springing of Ingrid Betancourt from a FARC camp in Colombia, the guerillas show they still have a taste for taking hostages.

Three tourists were taken hostage by FARC rebels while travelling by bus north of the town of Tulua on 14th September. Australian tourists Tod Simmonds (22) and Melanie Rose (21) were taken hostage along with an American nurse Emilia Gonzalez (19). In a method that is now quite standard for FARC, gunmen flagged down the bus and set up roadblocks in front and behind the vehicle. The hostages were then hustled into an SUV and driven away. Luis Sanchez, a passenger travelling on the bus, said later: "It was over very quickly. The FARC were not interested in any Colombians and we were all allowed to stay on the bus. They seemed to know what they were after." No one was hurt during the drama.

FARC, Latin America's longest-running insurgency, continues to hold an estimated 700 hostages. It has been facing renewed pressure to release its remaining hostages after people took to the streets in Colombia and around the world on 4th February to highlight the plight of its captives. Crowds gathered in 1000 towns and cities across Colombia, demanding the liberation of hundreds of hostages still held by FARC following the rescue of politician Ingrid Betancourt and 14 others on 2nd July.

FARC, surprisingly, does not enjoy a monopoly on hostage-taking in Colombia. The majority of the country's kidnappings are committed by common criminals who see the ransom monies as a lucrative addition to their income.

FROM TOP: Tod Simmonds, Melanie Rose and Emilia Gonzalez.

Department of the Navy • United States of America

PST = Pacific
Standard Time
SJ

Report of lieutenant Josh Coles from USS *Leviathan* regarding the interception off San Diego, CA, of a drugs submarine on 16th September 2008:

At 07:24 hours PST I received a message from Dolphin 261 chopper on routine coastal patrol that he had sighted a possible unauthorized submersible tracking northeast in sector Charlie 5 at a speed of 15 kt. Distance from *Leviathan* approximately 14 nm. I informed Captain Tippet and he ordered the *Leviathan* under way. ETA was expected to be 38 minutes. Sea conditions were: wind variable less than 10 kt. Wind waves 1 ft or less. Swell S 3 to 4 feet at 17 seconds.

At 08:15 hours we rendezvoused with Dolphin 261 which had maintained observation height over the submersible. Four crew and I, armed with side arms and automatic rifles, launched the inflatable and took position over the target. It was painted blue and clearly a Big Foot. It was moving at about 12 kt at a depth of 5 ft, its air-tube poking above the surface leaving a small wake. Given the calm conditions and clearness of the water we could see it quite clearly, but

A Big Foot is a self-propelled semi-submersible. These craft are increasingly being used to smuggle cocaine.   SJ

Dolphin helicopter as used by US customs to spot drug-smuggling operations   SJ

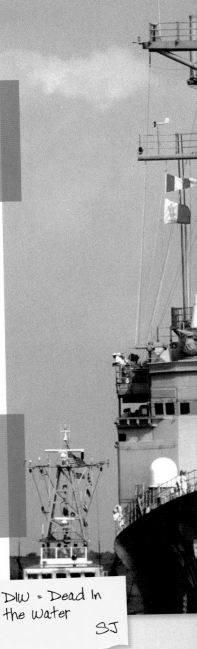

Department of the Navy • United States of America

there was no way of communicating with it. I radioed Captain Tippet and he ordered interdiction at my discretion.

I ordered petty officer Peters to fire a burst directly at the hull of the submersible. We could see the trace of bullets and them hitting the target. If the vessel was crewed (and we know some are controlled remotely) then they would be bound to hear the clatter on their hull. There was no change of course or depth from the vessel so we all fired at will. Again there was no change. I radioed the Captain and asked for the foredeck Bofors to be deployed across the submerged bows of the target.

Some 30 seconds later, after we had drawn back, there was the *flash-crack* of the Bofors gun and a plume of spray shot from the sea some 80 feet ahead of the submersible. If there were guys in that vessel they would have been scared witless by now. Sure enough a few minutes later the prow broke the surface followed by a low cabin with a square glass window. We pulled alongside and levelled our automatics at the window. There were two guys that we could see and they looked terrified. I used the megaphone and told them to hove to in English and then in Spanish. The vessel slowed until she was DIW. A hatch on the top of the cabin squealed open and a pair of hands appeared followed by a man in just a pair of denims – he kept his hands aloft, seeing the four assault rifles trained on him. There was a lot of shouting in Spanish (mostly foul language) before the second man appeared. I realized then that there was a third crew member on that boat who might be up to something unlawful. I jumped across to the hull of the sub while the two Spanish crew were

DIW = Dead In the Water

SJ

SEE TOP SECRET

US coastguard
cutter similar to
USS Leviathan
SJ

Department of the Navy • United States of America

H K – Heckler Koch USP compact 40mm
automatic favoured by US customs
SJ

transferred to the inflatable. When I looked into the cabin I saw the third crew member unscrewing the sub's seacocks in an attempt to scuttle her and water was pouring into the hull. I pointed my pistol at him and told him to stop. He threw a wrench at me which caught me on the arm. As he reached for an automatic I fired my H&K. There was no option. He slumped down by the steering gear his head almost under water. I propped him up against the bulkhead and was relieved to see he was still alive. The water was at waist height by now and I had to put my head under water to find the seacocks. When I came up for air I could hear Lieutenant Cash on the loud hailer telling me to get myself out of there and quick before the sub went down. I managed to close the seacocks, but the sub was lying very low in the water and it would only have taken a higher than normal wave to fill her up and send her down. I poked my head out of the hatch to make sure there was no one on the hull, slammed the hatch shut, sealed it and went down to the controls.

I'd been inside a narco sub before so I knew the general layout – trouble is they are all different. They are not made on an assembly line in Detroit. I had to start the engine before the pumps would work. The diesel engine spluttered to life when I found the start button. With the diesel running I knew that the sub was being pumped out so after a few minutes I was able to open the hatch again with safety. In those few minutes I realized what hot, filthy, smelly, disgusting tin cans these narco subs are. I almost pitied the man who had tried to kill me – he'd been in this hell-hole for days.

REPORT B REPORT C REPORT D REPORT E

PAGE B4

Big Foot – self-propelled semi-submersible 'Narco Sub'

This vessel is actually a semi submersible, so-called as it can't dive, and built illegally by drug traffickers to smuggle drugs. The subs vary in size and many can hold up to ten tonnes of cocaine. Equipped with diesel engines, they are typically made of fibreglass but can also be made from steel and are usually manned by a crew of four. They have large fuel tanks and can cover up to 3200 kilometres. These vessels travel just below the water's surface and many have twisted exhaust pipes that are only visible from the air. Ballast tanks allow the vessel's buoyancy to be altered. The crew live in cramped conditions as most of the internal area is designated for the drugs stash.

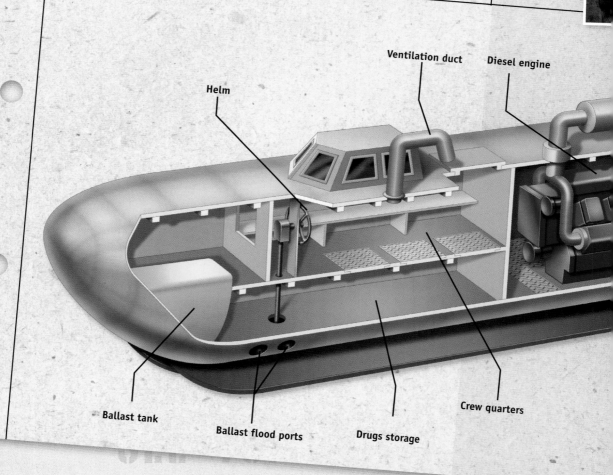

Helm

Ventilation duct   Diesel engine

Ballast tank

Ballast flood ports

Drugs storage

Crew quarters

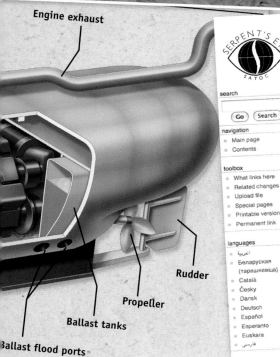

Some of the cocaine seized by US customs from the sub. These six packages weigh almost four kilos. After the final stage of processing turns it into cocaine hydrochloride, drug traffickers will ship the cocaine to the United States.
SJ

Engine exhaust

Rudder

Propeller

Ballast tanks

Ballast flood ports

article   edit this page   history

SERPENT'S EYE
SATOC

search

[Go] [Search]

navigation
- Main page
- Contents

toolbox
- What links here
- Related changes
- Upload file
- Special pages
- Printable version
- Permanent link

languages
- العربية
- Беларуская (тарашкевіца)
- Català
- Česky
- Dansk
- Deutsch
- Español
- Esperanto
- Euskara
- فارسی

The war on drugs

Coke users do more than just destroy the environment. They also fund the illegal groups that run the narcotics plantations and processing factories. Such gangs do not hesitate to maim, kill and generally terrorize local people to protect and promote their business. For instance, landmines are regularly placed around crops and processing labs to eliminate intruders. In 2008 in Colombia, such landmines killed almost 900 civilians. Right-wing paramilitaries are also frequently involved in drug trafficking. Kidnappings are also commonly undertaken in Colombia by narcotics groups. The Colombian Vice President, Francisco Santos Calderón, was himself kidnapped and held by a cocaine gang for eighteen months in the 1990s. And in July 2008 the French-Colombian politician Ingrid Betancourt was rescued in a spectacularly daring military mission after being held captive by FARC for six years. The FARC primarily profits from the drug trade by 'taxing' large coca growers and drug trafficking operations within territory that it controls, protecting cocaine processing labs and acting as a middleman between coca farmers and drug traffickers.

Since the election of hard-line President Alvaro Uribe in 2002, Colombia's government has stepped up efforts to tackle the trade. As a result, Colombia's government has prevented the sale of an estimated 377 tonnes of cocaine and wiped about $14 billion of global coke profits. However, it has been unable to seize control of the trade. This is why Calderón's office launched the Shared Responsibility project, designed to encourage consumer countries to participate in the fight against coca production. Whether these efforts will be successful remains to be seen.

GDP - Gross Domestic Product per capita is an indicator of the standard of living in an economy per head.

SJ

SERPENT'S EYE
SATOC

Memo to SATOC Re: Lt. Coles' report

SE/DD25908

Over eight metric tonnes of cocaine was found behind a welded section of the hull when the submersible was brought back to San Diego. Forensics ascertained that the sample they analyzed had the trademark composition of a factory near Aguachica – very much FARC territory. The factory is run by one of the most powerful drug lords in Colombia: Estafan Peron.

The drug smuggler who was shot by Coles recovered from his wounds, but would not name Peron. Neither would the other two, though it is likely that they would have met him. Peron has instilled absolute loyalty in his workforce through fear. In the past, he has ordered henchmen to kill or torture family members and/or close associates of a betrayer before killing the person in question. Witnesses under protective custody have been found and killed before they could give evidence. Members of his vast network of criminals have even managed to kill betrayers serving prison sentences. His hired assassins are called 'sicarios' and their favoured method of killing is quiet and slow – the garrotte. There are fewer killings these days because no one dares betray him.

This is the power of the unimaginable wealth gained from drug trafficking. In Colombia as a whole the drugs trade is thought to be worth over a billion dollars, but it is locked up in over a million hectares of land, in housing schemes, in newspapers, and hundreds of other apparently legitimate businesses. As for Peron's personal wealth, it's anyone's guess – perhaps a fifth of the billion dollars. That buys a lot of unquestioning obedience. The per capita GDP in Colombia is just over $6000. Half the population is below the poverty line. The temptation for an unemployed banana picker to venture into the dangerous but potentially lucrative world of drugs is huge. Once in though, there's no getting out.

Colonel Davies

San Diego Police loading packages of cocaine seized from the Esperanza semi-sub.

SJ

Cocaine users are snorting the rainforest

Colombia's Vice President, Francisco Santos Calderón, has appealed to cocaine users across the world to consider the impact of their habit on the environment. "Every user that snorts a gram of cocaine kills 4.4 square metres of rainforest," he told police officers at a 2008 conference in Belfast, Northern Ireland.

According to Calderón, 300,000 hectares of tropical rainforest are destroyed each year to make way for coca plants and the industrial chemicals needed to turn them into a value-added product. Colombia has cultivated the bulk of the world's cocaine for decades – UN figures in 2008 estimate the country's share of global production at more than 60%. The clearing of Colombian land for coca crops has had a devastating ecological impact on one of the world's most bio-diverse areas, risking extinction for irreplaceable species of flora and fauna. The armed groups operating in forested areas have also decimated wildlife for food and target practice. Meanwhile, the chemicals used to process the leaves have been dumped in waterways, causing widespread pollution of the river system, threatening the existence of thousands of species and also indigenous rainforest peoples. Of course, deforestation is also a major contributor to global warming . In recent years, it has been responsible for about one-fifth of worldwide CO_2 emissions. This is more

A coca field in La Macarena National Park, Meta

Photo: Colombia Journal

than the amount produced by the whole of the global transport sector annually (Stern, 2006).

While Calderón appreciates that being aware of green issues will not persuade addicts to give up, it might make middle-class social users change their minds about their recreational use. He said, "For somebody who drives a hybrid, who recycles, who is worried about global warming – to tell him that a night of partying will destroy 4-m-square of rainforest might lead him to make another decision."

In the last 15 years, Colombia has lost more than two million hectares of rainforest to plant coca. "The rainforest is not just Colombian," Calderón added. "It belongs to all of us who live on this planet. So we should all be worried about it."

Britain's coke habit

- UK Home Office figures show that in 2008 around 810,000 people in Britain used cocaine.

- Over the past decade, the proportion of adults in the UK using cocaine has almost quadrupled, from 0.6% in 1996 to 2.3% in 2007.

- In 2008, the UK had the highest number of cocaine users in the European Union.

- Cocaine and heroin use cost the British economy around £1bn a year in health and crime bills.

Evening *Times* | 21st September 2008

Two of three Colombia hostages released

L ate last night the Australian embassy in Bogotá issued a statement saying that two of the three hostages abducted on 14th September had been released safely into their hands by FARC rebels. Tod Simmonds (22) and his girlfriend Melanie Rose (21) were still bound and blindfolded when they were found by Colombian soldiers 1.5 kilometres from the agreed rendezvous point. It was not disclosed why the tourists were released, but it is suspected that several FARC members currently in custody may be released some time this week. The fate of Emilia Gonzalez (19) who was taken hostage at the same time is not known.

Nick Finlay, the US Senator seized by FARC rebels in February of this year, is believed to be held by the same group. The whereabouts of the camp is unknown but is believed to be in forested area 200 kilometres north of Medellin. FARC camps are moved all the time to avoid discovery by the Colombian army. Satellite photography has made hiding the camps a serious problem for the rebels though cover from the rainforest canopy makes detection for the security forces extremely difficult.

A photo from archives of a stream in Colombia polluted by coca farmers.   SJ

Col. D. Davies

23.09.2008
SE/DD26308

A recent photo of
Will Sugden from
archives.

File note from

I was contacted by Will Sugden, SATOC Recruitment Officer for Australia and the
Far East. He called me late last night from his Sydney office and said that he had
managed to speak to the two Australian tourists, Tod Simmonds and Melanie Rose,
taken hostage at the same time as Gonzalez. They are now at the Australian embassy
in Bogotá. Rose was kept in the same hut as Gonzalez for the duration of her
imprisonment. She confirmed that Gonzalez's iPhone was seized immediately, just as
we anticipated. However, when one of the guards found that he could not make a call
when he took it within range of a beacon, he got suspicious. They are not above
torturing Gonzalez if they think she has information that will be of use to them. The
iPhone will continue to transmit its signal as long as it has charge. Of course, if the
signal is to be used to locate the camp, the iPhone must stay on site.

The SE iPhone has two sim cards, one dummy
one and one built into the circuitry of the phone.
This one pulses a GPS signal every 30 minutes,
even if the phone is turned off, to allow us to
pinpoint its location by satellite.

SJ

The 'cocina', where
the hostages were
forced to work.
SJ

REPORT A

SERPENT'S EYE
SATOC

SE/DD26408

'crook' – Australian slang for ill. SJ

Transcript of conference call Sugden made to Simmonds and Rose: 22.09.2008, 20:49

Sugden asks if they saw or heard anything of Finlay while in the camp.

Simmonds: On our third day Melanie was put on cooking duties and I was taken from the hut and led through jungle to a cocaine kitchen. My job was to carry five gallon plastic tanks of used chemicals like benzene and hydrochloric acid to a stream and tip in the liquid. The stream stank like paint thinners. It was back-breaking work in the heat and the chemicals were very toxic – they made me spew and cough and burnt my eyes. Anyway, I got these full plastic containers from a long shed where the cocaine was prepared and that's where I saw someone who looked a bit like Finlay. I saw photos of him in the press when he was taken hostage. This guy could have been him, but he had a long beard, long hair and his skin, it was almost yellow. He looked crook, that guy. Effect of the chemicals I guess. Or they may have him hooked on crack. That's what the sickos do to some of the hostages.

He is probably referring to benzene or possibly toluene – both are used to extract cocaine from coca leaves. SJ

Sugden to Rose: Tell me what you know about Miss Gonzalez, the other hostage taken from your bus.

Rose: I first got to know Em on the bus to Bogotá. We hit it off right away – that can happen sometimes when you're travelling and it's a really special moment. Em was lovely, and completely fearless as well. A 19-year-old girl travelling alone in Colombia – well, you wouldn't recommend it, you know? I know she had a friend back near the border she was getting medicine for, so she had to do it, I guess, but still. (Pauses) Me and Todd were treated kind of different from the others. I think they didn't plan to keep us more than a few days. Maybe they don't like Aussies. Too much bloody trouble. (Laughs)

Sugden: Were you in the same hut as Gonzalez?

Rose: Most of the time. On the first full day she was taken away for questioning. I don't know what they did to her, but she looked different when she came back after two days of it, I can tell you.

A leech, after feeding on a foot. SJ

SERPENT'S EYE · SATOC

Sugden: In what way?

Rose: She was very distant. She didn't look as though they'd hit her, but there were bruises on her arms and ankles where she'd been manacled. I reckon she was drugged with something, but she wouldn't say anything about what had happened. And her feet were sore, she found it difficult to walk.

Sugden: Tell me about the camp.

'Dunnies' - Australian slang for toilets. SJ

Rose: It was basic, the dunnies were just holes in the ground, we were allowed to wash in the stream. It was alive with leeches, but at least it was upstream from the cocina. There were four huts where the guards slept and three huts – just shelters really – where the hostages were kept at night. I think Finlay was held in a seperate hut somewhere on the other side of the camp. I was in one with Em and three Colombian women who'd been held for months. Tod was in a shelter with four guys – all of them from the Colombian army. The guys were handcuffed to the walls of the shelter every night, weren't you, Tod?

Simmonds: That was the worst bit for me. If I did sleep I woke up with pins and needles. The girls weren't handcuffed – guess the guards had some chivalry. Not that you'd get far if you went walkabout – it was thick jungle and each night they took our shoes away.

Sugden: Can you tell me anything else about camp security?

Simmonds: The entrance was by a track and that was carefully guarded. Everything was really well hidden that's for sure. Hardly saw much blue sky because of solid tree cover. They were paranoid about being spotted by satellites or helicopters. And when they walked us to the cocaine kitchen we were blindfolded so we wouldn't see any landmarks. The guards were armed to the teeth all the time and one or two seemed like they were itching to use their rifles or pistols or machetes. I tried not to catch their eyes.

Sugden: Did they send out patrols?

Simmonds: There were patrols coming and going all the time. Patrols would come in and

Archive photos of workers in a 'cocina'.
SJ

Processing coca leaves in a cocina.

The patch on Rosco's neck is probably Leichmaniasis – a flesh-eating disease caused by parasites, transmitted by the bite of certain species of sand fly. It is estimated that nearly 13,000 cases of the disease were recorded in Colombia throughout 2004.

SJ

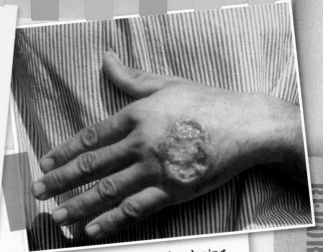

SATOC

take over from the guards to get rest I suppose – and stop any relationships developing with the hostages.

Sugden: When did you last see Gonzalez?

Rose: I saw her on the last day we were held there. She looked a bit better, more like her old self. She told me the FARC were negotiating with her lawyer on some huge ransom deal. Soon after that Rosco came into the hut.

Sugden: Who is Rosco?

Rose: He's a maggot, that's what he is. An evil little man with piggy eyes and a patch of rotten flesh on his neck. He's the chief interrogator. He had blood on his hands – I mean literally. There was blood on his knuckles and he was proud of it. He told us that we would be released soon, but not Em. He said, "She's been a very naughty girl so I've had to give her little smack." And then he smiled at me with his brown teeth.

Harvested coca leaves before processing.

SERPENT'S EYE
SATOC

Col. D. Davies

23.09.2008
SE/DD26452

* See attached profile on Pedro Mori.
SJ

File note from Col. Davies

I contacted Abbot and told him that Finlay had been located. I'd allowed for this operation to take two, possibly three, months, but I decided that we had to speed things up. Finlay was clearly sick and it seemed Gonzalez was in imminent danger – it was possible that Rosco had discovered the transmitter in her iPhone.

I instructed Abbot to contact Pedro Mori. Mori has been a sleeper for SATOC since 2002. He was badly injured in 2005 when a FARC roadside bomb exploded. Others in his squad were not so lucky (see attached). I know he will relish this chance to be woken up.

Colombian rebels kill nine police

Newspaper clipping of the aftermath of the roadside bomb that killed Mori's colleagues.

SJ

At least nine Colombian policemen have been killed and six others injured by a roadside bomb in Santander province.

The authorities say it was planted by the FARC left-wing rebel group near Landazuri, 160 kilometres north of the capital, Bogotá.

The policemen were taking part in a mission to destroy coca bushes, which supply the raw material for cocaine, a key source of income for the rebels.

Correspondents say it is the worst guerrilla attack this year in Colombia.

The dead were members of a police unit based in the north-eastern city of Bucaramanga.

The attack is another blow for President Alvaro Uribe, who has vowed to crush the rebels by the end of his term in 2010.

Archive photo of
Mori training with
British Special
Forces in Belize.
SJ

SERPENT'S EYE
SATOC

Profile on Pedro Mori

DOB 17.11.1965

Pedro Carlos Mori

Family Parents: Cesar Mori, Gloria Torres

Education A bi-lingual school in Barranquilla, then Atlantico University, degree in politics.

Career Born in Arauca. Joined the Colombian Army in 1987 where he excelled at his Lancero training*. Rose to rank of captain in 15th Mobile Brigade. In 1990 he moved to a GAULA unit (Spanish for Unified Action Groups for Personal Freedom) which specialized in hostage release. He was involved in action against FARC on many occasions, distinguishing himself in battle.

He left the army in 1992 and joined the Colombian Police – a difficult move as there are often tensions between the two services. He became involved in a move to clean up the force. For years the police had been suspected of complicity with drugs barons and FARC.

In 2005 a roadside bomb, presumed to have been planted by FARC, killed 14 policemen. Mori was badly wounded but survived. It took him a year to recover from his injuries.

SEE He was contacted by Dan Thorpe of our recruitment division and readily agreed to become a sleeper. He has developed a small but highly effective cell of contacts, mostly with military experience. His unique background and huge likeability allow him to draw support from both the military and the police.

---

*A Lancero training course in counterinsurgency warfare is held in Tolemaida, 240 kilometres from Bogotá, where temperatures range between 29.5–38°C throughout the year. The course, which has been called the toughest in the world, employs severe techniques and live ammunition. Because of its exceptional nature, the course has gained international prestige.

SATOC INFOBASE
FILE: 456V

SE iPhone with tracker modification

The SE iPhone has some special features but it hides its secrets well. If the obvious SIM card is removed, the secondary SIM card will continue doing its job secretly, providing pulses every 30 minutes to reveal its location.

Plastic casing

3.7 volt Li-Lon polymer phone battery

Main SIM card

Hidden SIM card

Logic board

I've seen the beasts in the jungle
Heard their blood-chilling calls
Seen their famished eyes
I've watched the beasts in the jungle
Watched them kill without a care
And feed on hate-soaked lies

I've been a beast in the jungle
Tasted blood, iron and salt
Felt my hate burn with a forest fire heat

And I will flee the beasts of the jungle
Escape their teeth and claws of rage
With running strides and dancing feet.

We file SE jottings and personal notes to give us an insight into the psychological pressures they have endured. This poem was part of Gonzalez's journal.

SJ

Abbot's journal

<u>25 Sept</u> : Hotel doesn't get any better. After two weeks here I'm calling the roaches by their pet names. The food's not bad though — Rocky and Bugsy seem to enjoy the chunchullo! Received a com from D to say that I'm to go to Bogotá and rendez with a Pedro Mori. My flight is from Pasto tomorrow — early.

<u>26 Sept</u>: Travelled to Pasto last night. Stopped the chiva at a random crossroads outside Pasto and got off, glancing at the passengers as I left, trying to pick out any shadows. Noticed a glimmer of panic on one young guy's face as he realized I was leaving, but he stayed put. I waited until the chiva disappeared into the distance. He would have been on his cell phone calling for back-up by then. No doubt he'd figured that I was going to the airport, but I wasn't going to make it easy for them.

Chunchullo is a Colombian dish of grilled or fried pork, beef, or lamb small intestine.

SJ

Chiva buses

article | edit this page | history

The most common mode of public transport in rural Colombia has long been the chiva bus (or *escaleras*). These vehicles are brightly decorated with patterns and figures, usually in the colours of the flag of Colombia. Inside, people sit on wooden benches, while outside a ladder gives access to a rack on the roof for carrying more passengers, livestock and luggage. Each bus is usually given a nickname by the driver or owner.

However, today chivas have become popular as party buses in big cities such as Cartagena. The inside space, with the benches sometimes removed, is filled with a bar, a band and disco lights – sometimes even a smoke machine! The bus drives from bar to bar, picking up and dropping off partygoers who drink and dance the night away. Each bus has a 'director' with a microphone who leads the fun.

SERPENT'S EYE · SATOC

search

Go | Search

navigation
- Main page
- Contents

toolbox
- What links here
- Related changes
- Upload file
- Special pages
- Printable version
- Permanent link

languages
- العربية

New Message   Cancel

To: **R**

Wait for cab co. 'Santa Fe'. Driver will bring you to me + lose shadows. —Paternoster5

Send

Operator's signatures (call signs), change each day. They are contacted by head office to confirm each day's call sign.

SJ

Aeropuerto El Dorado

Cl 26 (Autopista El Dora

Ac 86 (Cuidad de Cali)

PM = Pedro Mori

<u>27 Sept:</u> I received a text from PM when I was waiting for a cab at Bogota airport. He had the right call sign for the day, so I felt confident it was genuine. A Santa Fe cab pulled up beside me as I reached the front of the line — the driver must have counted the number of people waiting and positioned himself in the line of cabs accordingly. He was a fit-looking guy in his early forties who gave me a searching look. As we pulled away I realized the cab was not a lumbering, smoking Nissan like most of the cabs in Colombia — no sir. We shot out of the airport like a bat outta hell — screamed down the Autopista El Dorado at over 90 mph, flew past the Botanical Gardens, where the Polizia just looked on as we scorched past them. The driver threw a violent u-turn in the Congreso Eucaristico and swerved into a nest of alleyways in the Barrios Unidos, causing people to jump into doorways. The cab plunged down a steep driveway that took us into a dark underground garage, and finally screeched to a halt inches from a concrete wall. The driver killed the engine and sat silent for all of a minute while my heart pounded painfully against my ribs. I started to say something but he silenced me with a finger to his lips. At last he said, "OK, I think we lost them." He held out his hand and said, "Pedro Mori. How's that old fox Duffy? Still drinking that disgusting Spanish brandy?"

B O

Archive photo of street
in Bogota leading to
the underground garage.
It is no wider than
a car!

SJ

REPORT A

REPORT B

Turns out Pedro had taken no chances with us being tailed. The traffic police were friends of his — as soon as they'd let him speed through Bogota they stopped the following traffic for three or four minutes. Any tail would have been caught up in the chaos. Pedro said he gave FARC the utmost respect — the same respect he'd give a lunatic with a chainsaw. He told me that we needed to move quickly, and that Duffy was worried about Emilia as well as Finlay. We would be driving to Barrancabermeja tonight. I took out my SE iPhone and tuned it to the signal from the tracker in Em's iPhone. It read the same as it had for two weeks — a blinking blue dot on a Google Earth map a few miles south of Zaragoza. I stared at the dot and thought of Em, not wanting to imagine what might be happening to her. Her last communication with me, nearly three weeks ago, had been <3 — a text heart.

A Nissan Patrol in jungle colours was parked in the same garage. We transferred to this and drove out of Bogota, heading north on main highway 50.

It was clear that there was a growing attachment between Abbot and Gonzalez - not unusual in dangerous and stressful circumstances.
SJ

iPhone transmitter

Estimated location of FARC camp

Alarmingly, for a day or so the iPhone signal transmitted from a position some distance from the estimated location of the FARC camp. Turned out the guard was searching for a better signal.
SJ

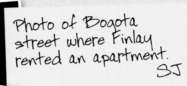

Photo of Bogota
street where Finlay
rented an apartment.
SJ

Useful phrases

Gonzalez had fluent
Spanish, but Abbot's
needed polishing

68

Hola *(ola)*: . . . . .Hello

Buenos dias *(bwoo nas deeas)*: . . . . .Good day

Buenos tardes *(bwoo nas tar des)*: . . . . .Good afternoon

Buenos noches *(bwoo nas no ches)*: . . . . .Good night *or* good evening

Mucho gusto *(much o goos toe)*: . . . . .Pleased to meet you

Me llamo . . . *(meh yah moh...)*: . . . . .My name is…

Como se llama? *(com o say ya ma)*: . . . . .What's your name?

Como esta usted? *(como es ta oost ed)*: . . . . .How are you (polite)?

Que tal? *(kay tal)*: . . . . .How are you? (informal)

Muy bien, gracias *(mooey byehn, grah syahss)*: . . . . .I am fine, thank you.

De donde eres? *(de don day err ez)*: . . . . .Where are you from?

Perdona *(per donna)*: . . . . .Excuse me

Habla usted ingles? *(Ah blah oo steth een gles?)*: . . . .Do you speak English?

Me puede ayudar? *(meh poo eh deh ah yoo dar?)*: . . . .Can you help me?

Quisiera . . . *(key sea era...)*: . . . . .I would like…

Una cerveza *(oona ser vay sah)*: . . . . .a beer

Un bocadillo *(oon bock a di yo)*: . . . . .a sandwich

Cuanto cuesta? *(kwan toh kwes tah)*: . . . . .How much is it?

Tiene la hora? *(tee any la ora)*: . . . . .Do you have the time?

Donde esta la parada del autobus?
(don day es ta la par ada del ow toe bus): . . . . .Where is the bus stop?

Tengo un problema/un dolor
(ten go oon pro blame a/oon doll or): . . . . .I have a problem/a pain

Hay una farmacia cerca?
(Eye oona farm a thee a ser ca): . . . . .Is there a chemist's nearby?

Donde esta el bano? *(don day es ta el bano)*: . . . . . . .Where is the toilet?

Estoy perdido *(es toy per dee do)*: . . . . .I'm lost

Lo siento *(low see en toe)*: . . . . .I'm sorry

No lo se *(no lo say)*: . . . . .I don't understand

No entiendo *(noh ehn tyehn doh)*: . . . . .I don't understand

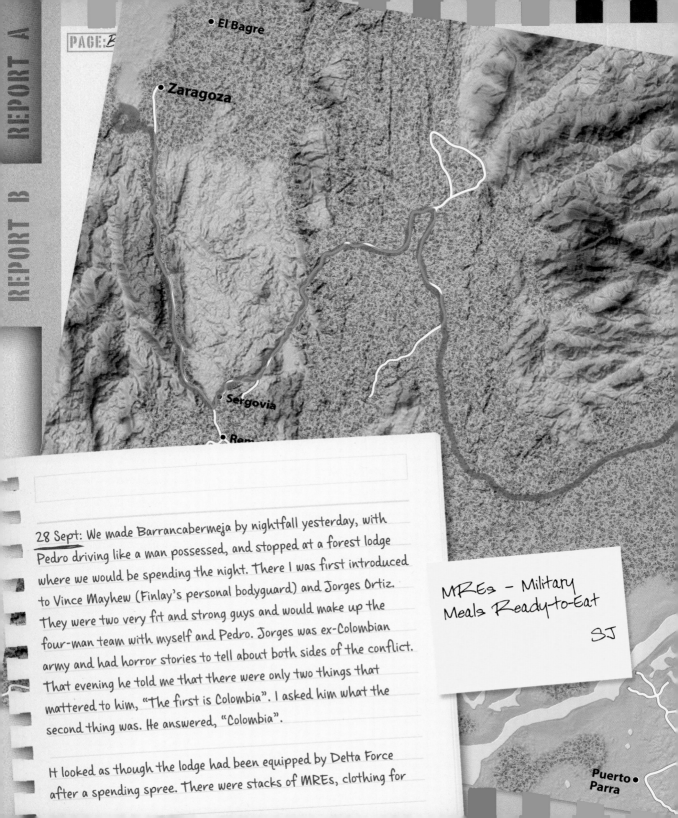

• El Bagre

• **Zaragoza**

• **Sergovia**

• Rem...

Puerto Parra

28 Sept: We made Barrancabermeja by nightfall yesterday, with Pedro driving like a man possessed, and stopped at a forest lodge where we would be spending the night. There I was first introduced to Vince Mayhew (Finlay's personal bodyguard) and Jorges Ortiz. They were two very fit and strong guys and would make up the four-man team with myself and Pedro. Jorges was ex-Colombian army and had horror stories to tell about both sides of the conflict. That evening he told me that there were only two things that mattered to him, "The first is Colombia". I asked him what the second thing was. He answered, "Colombia".

It looked as though the lodge had been equipped by Delta Force after a spending spree. There were stacks of MREs, clothing for

MREs – Military
Meals Ready-to-Eat

SJ

the jungle, first aid packs, machetes, climbing gear, an inflatable with outboard, emergency shelters, camo face paint, wire saws, a wonderful thermal imaging camera, you name it. Standard SAS weaponry was in abundance: The Heckler and Koch HK33KE assault rifle with short barrel and collapsible stock, Sig Sauer P230 hand gun, flash-bang stun grenades, even an RPG.

Zaragoza was another 70 miles, which on these roads could take a day or more. Pedro spread out a map and traced the route we would be taking. "It's a lousy road. We'll take the four wheel drive to here and hide her from view. Then it's on foot through jungle to the FARC camp, which is here. There is a rough track that goes right into the camp, but we can't take that unless we want to give the game away. We'll reconnoitre for a day, possibly two, and decide how to proceed when we're there. Tomorrow we check the equipment and do some weapons practice. When did you last do jungle training?" I told him that Em and I had spent two months with Special Forces in Belize only a month before getting this assignment. "Good," he said, "but you'll still need practice. Now we get some sleep." I had a load of questions but I was too exhausted to ask them, or to even brush away the ravenous mosquitoes as darkness, jungle sounds and sleep engulfed me.

Satellite image of the terrain west of Barrancabermeja.

SJ

REPORT A

REPORT B

Standard operational weaponry

Rocket-propelled grenade (RPG): A hand-held, shoulder-launched anti-tank weapon capable of firing an unguided rocket equipped with an explosive warhead. RPGs are effective against lightly armoured vehicles such as armoured personnel carriers (APCs) or unarmoured wheeled vehicles, as well as against buildings and bunkers.

Sig Sauer P230: Handgun, holding 9 rounds.

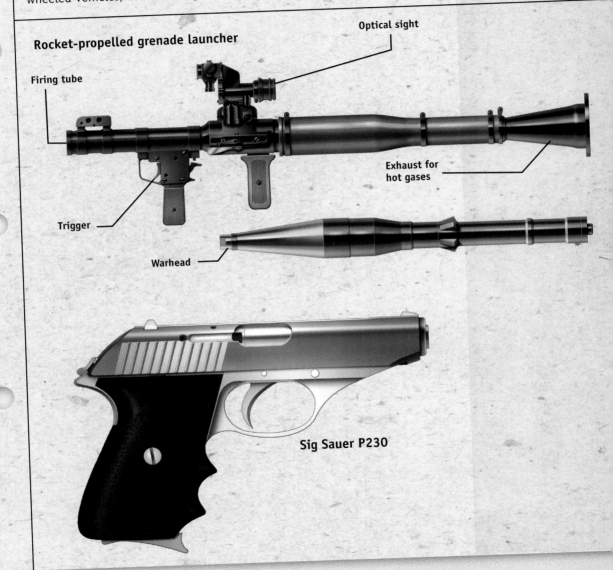

Rocket-propelled grenade launcher

Optical sight

Firing tube

Exhaust for hot gases

Trigger

Warhead

Sig Sauer P230

HK33: 5.56 mm assault rifle developed in the 1960s by West German armament manufacturer Heckler & Koch GmbH (H&K) primarily for export.

M84 stun grenade: The current issue stun grenade of the US Army. Contains a mix of ammonium and magnesium. Upon detonation it emits a blinding flash of several million candela and 170 dB of noise. Exposure to this without ear/eye protection can lead to temporary blindness and hearing damage. Can cause an explosion if detonated in the presence of fumes or gases.

Heckler and Koch HK33 assault rifle

M84 stun grenade

SERPENT'S EYE
SATOC

search

[Go] [Search]

navigation
- Main page
- Contents

toolbox
- What links here
- Related changes
- Upload file
- Special pages
- Printable version
- Permanent link

languages
- العربية
- Беларуская (тарашкевіца)
- Català
- Česky
- Dansk
- Deutsch
- Español
- Esperanto
- Euskara
- فارسی

article | edit this page | history

Military MRE (Meals-Ready-to-Eat)

A United States Military MRE is a totally self-contained complete meal, made up of a main course and a number of other food and drink items. One MRE provides an average of 1250 calories (13% protein, 36% fat and 51% carbohydrates) and gives one-third of the Military Recommended Daily Allowance of vitamins and minerals. Three MREs comprise a full day's nutritional needs. MREs are the main operational food ration for the United States Armed Forces. (The British military use a 24-hour Operational Ration Pack.)

A typical MRE would include:
- A main course eg chilli or stew
- A side dish eg rice or mash
- Bread or a cracker and some type of spread
- Dessert eg cookies or fruit
- Sweets or chocolate
- Drinks eg squash, cocoa, milkshakes, coffee, tea
- Accessories eg spoon, salt, sugar, matches, creamer, chewing gum, toilet paper

All the contents of an MRE can be eaten without cooking, though most soldiers agree that if you are able to heat up the main dishes, it vastly improves the taste. Each MRE contains a flameless ration heater, which is activated by water to heat up food.

The packaging of MREs is designed to withstand rough conditions, such as parachute drops, and exposure to the elements. The meals are designed to have a shelf life of three years when stored at 80°F.

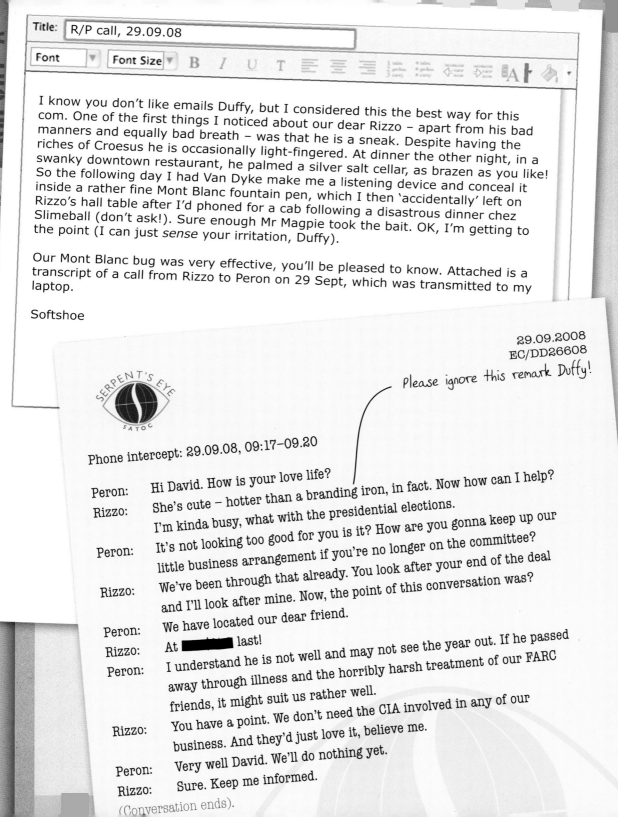

Title: R/P call, 29.09.08

I know you don't like emails Duffy, but I considered this the best way for this com. One of the first things I noticed about our dear Rizzo – apart from his bad manners and equally bad breath – was that he is a sneak. Despite having the riches of Croesus he is occasionally light-fingered. At dinner the other night, in a swanky downtown restaurant, he palmed a silver salt cellar, as brazen as you like! So the following day I had Van Dyke make me a listening device and conceal it inside a rather fine Mont Blanc fountain pen, which I then 'accidentally' left on Rizzo's hall table after I'd phoned for a cab following a disastrous dinner chez Slimeball (don't ask!). Sure enough Mr Magpie took the bait. OK, I'm getting to the point (I can just *sense* your irritation, Duffy).

Our Mont Blanc bug was very effective, you'll be pleased to know. Attached is a transcript of a call from Rizzo to Peron on 29 Sept, which was transmitted to my laptop.

Softshoe

29.09.2008
EC/DD26608

Please ignore this remark Duffy!

SERPENT'S EYE
SATOC

Phone intercept: 29.09.08, 09:17–09.20

Peron:	Hi David. How is your love life?
Rizzo:	She's cute – hotter than a branding iron, in fact. Now how can I help? I'm kinda busy, what with the presidential elections.
Peron:	It's not looking too good for you is it? How are you gonna keep up our little business arrangement if you're no longer on the committee?
Rizzo:	We've been through that already. You look after your end of the deal and I'll look after mine. Now, the point of this conversation was?
Peron:	We have located our dear friend.
Rizzo:	At ▓▓▓▓▓ last!
Peron:	I understand he is not well and may not see the year out. If he passed away through illness and the horribly harsh treatment of our FARC friends, it might suit us rather well.
Rizzo:	You have a point. We don't need the CIA involved in any of our business. And they'd just love it, believe me.
Peron:	Very well David. We'll do nothing yet.
Rizzo:	Sure. Keep me informed.

(Conversation ends).

The modified Mont Blanc listening device was based on a Russian-designed spying tool developed in the Cold War. Using the latest miniaturization technology, Van Dyke (technical division) linked the transmitting signal to local cell phone networks thus increasing transmission range and saving battery life.

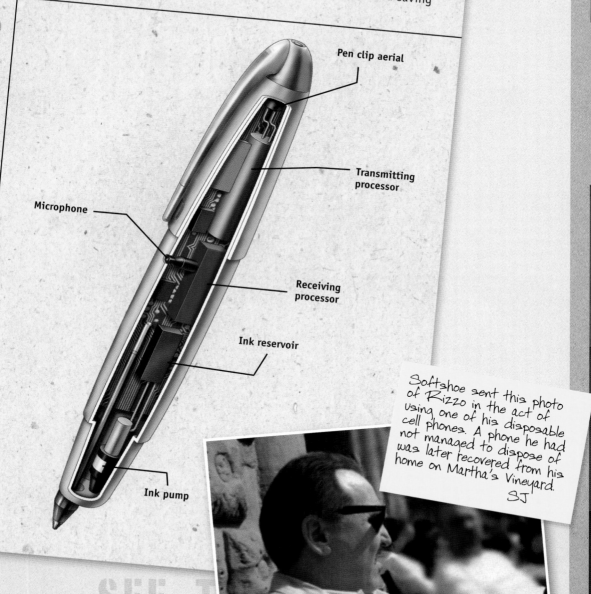

Pen clip aerial

Transmitting processor

Microphone

Receiving processor

Ink reservoir

Ink pump

Softshoe sent this photo of Rizzo in the act of using one of his disposable cell phones. A phone he had not managed to dispose of was later recovered from his home on Martha's Vineyard.
SJ

REPORT B

REPORT C

REPORT D

REPORT E

SPECIAL FORCES EQUIPMENT

Binoculars
Maximum brightness in low light conditions.

Pocket knife
All-in-one 11 cm pocket tool.

Mess tins
Aluminium 2-piece set.

Light-emitting diode torch
Extreme and reliable directional beam.

Map compass lensatic
Comprises swivel dial, magnifying glass, adjustable viewer, magnetic compass needle, sighting wire and folding metal casing.

First-aid kit
Designed for extreme use in adverse conditions.

Basha
Waterproof canvas sheet with eyelets. This can be used as a shelter, in the form of an impromptu tent or groundsheet.

Spent this morning checking equipment and packing our bergens. SE training makes you thorough, but Pedro is beyond thorough! He's the kind of guy you need when it comes to hostile terrain peopled by hostile bad guys, believe me. We went jungle-side and found a clearing — one of the many left by coca eradication schemes. Jorges painted a figure on a piece of man-sized tenting canvas and hung it from a tree. The drill was that we all had to run 50 yards, zig-zag fashion, and nail the canvas-man with HK33s. I did OK I am pleased to record. "You got that son-of-a-tent real good Ricky boy. That is one dead tent man," Pedro told me and I felt I'd just won a major battle single-handed. When he did his pass running low and fast, he hit the canvas with at least twice as many shots in a tight grouping. We leave in about two hours' time.

SJ

Mori was always an excellent shot.

550 Parachute cord
A 550-pound test-strength cord useful for securing equipment, making traps and shelter construction.

300g Army bergen 75 litre
Made from durable polyester that has been coated to give water-resistant properties.

CHECKLIST FOR SPECIAL FORCES CLOTHING

- ☐ Flame retardant carbonized viscose undergarments
- ☐ One-piece assault suit made of flame-retardant Nomex 3
- ☐ Fireproof knee and elbow pads
- ☐ Bullet-proof armoured waistcoat designed to stop a round and also absorb its kinetic energy
- ☐ Ceramic armour plates covering the front, back and groin
- ☐ AC100 armoured helmet able to stop a 9mm round at close range
- ☐ SF10 respirator providing protection against CS and CN gas and smoke. The sf10 incorporates anti-flash lenses, internal mic and interfaces for external oxygen supply and radio systems. It can be fitted with filters for protection from chemical and biological attacks
- ☐ Assault vest and harness featuring magazine pouches and rings for attaching stun and tear gas grenades
- ☐ Abseil harness featuring special rings for hooking up to ropes
- ☐ Respirator pouch — sometimes carried although in most circumstances the gas mask will be will shoved up a trooper's arm when not worn
- ☐ Radio harness — each assaulter is wired with a radio mic and earpiece
- ☐ Breaching gear

images supplied by www.silvermans.co.uk

REPORT B
REPORT C
REPORT D
REPORT E

SERPENT'S EYE
SATOC

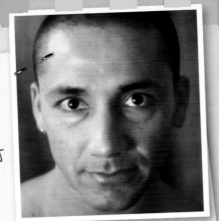

Picar's challenging stare caught on a prison security camera in 2001. SJ

Profile on Juan Picar

Juan Pablo Picar **DOB** 02.05.1976, Cartago

Parents Lina Picar (father not known)

Education Pereira, Colegio Americano until 1992

Career Moved to Medellin and became involved in drug dealing. Held by police on suspicion of the murder of 15-year-old Rosa Ostina, June 1995. Released due to lack of evidence. Tried and convicted for murder of a rival gang member in 1999, Picar was sentenced to life imprisonment. He served 18 months at Le Modelo Prison (nr Bogotá) before escaping during a mass breakout. Believed to be a senior member of the Red Hawks cocaine gang based in Bogotá.

Location His exact whereabouts have been unclear since 2005. Then, he was believed to be working with ex-paramilitary Jose Carraberos, a known assassin, on behalf of Estafan Peron in Northwest highlands.

Category Extremely dangerous, treat with caution.

Favoured killing methods Garrotte, Mauser K98

Weaknesses A lack of control under pressure. Bloodlust. Cruelty.

These bolas were found by Abbot in a market in Ipiales. They are used by gauchos to bring down cattle for branding etc. Picar is known to use them so his victims are alive when he catches them! SJ

*Enrigues Rosco, chief interrogator for FARC in Northwest and on the take from Peron. Undoubted psychopath who enjoys his work. This photo was taken in May 2007.

SJ*

call made by Picar to Peron

SERPENT'S EYE
SATOC

Phone intercept: 29.09.08, 18:38–18:42 (original was Spanish)

He is referring to Rosco

Peron: Yes?

Picar: Good day Señor Peron. That little FARC pig has been squealing.

Peron: And? This is a secure line, Juan, you can speak freely.

Picar: Good. I met with Rosco this morning. He would not say much about Finlay – only that he will not last long at the rate he is deteriorating. He also mentioned an American girl he has taken hostage. He is holding her at the Zaragoza camp. He said the girl had an iPhone that had some unusual features.

Peron: Is this leading somewhere, Juan?

Picar: Sure, sure. Rosco thought it might contain a tracking device or a miniature transmitter. I asked if he would let me see it, but he said it had been stolen, all the guards want an iPhone. The pig is lying. He tortured the girl of course, but so far she has told him nothing of any value. He does not want to kill her or maim her permanently because he thinks he will get a good ransom for her.

Peron: You think she may have been sent there on purpose? Who would willingly become a hostage to FARC?

Picar: I think we should bring our plan forward. We can't just wait for Finlay to die of natural causes – it may take months, no matter that Rosco works him like a horse and feeds him like a mouse.

Peron: Very well. How quickly can you be ready?

Picar: Give me a day. Two at most.

Peron: Very well.

(Conversation ends).

SERPENT'S EYE

SATOC

SEE TOP SECRET

REPORT C: OBJECTIVES

1. Locate targets and establish contact.

2. Formulate plan in situ to free targets safely and with minimum bloodshed.

REPORT C

REPORT D

REPORT E

FARC Information and statistics

FARC guerrillas in their camp in the Colombian jungle

Full name: The Revolutionary Armed Forces of Colombia

Description: Arguably the most powerful and richest rebel army in the world.

Origin: Originally a band of 14 armed rebels formed in 1964 by uneducated peasant Manuel 'Sureshot' Marulanda (real name: Pedro Antonio Marin), it became the military wing of the Colombian Communist Party.

Aim: To overthrow the government and establish a Marxist regime.

Organization: Governed by a secretariat led by Alfonso Cano and six others, since the death of Marulanda from a heart attack in 2008. (He had survived over 40 years of attempts by the Colombian government to assassinate him.) The FARC is organized along military lines and members wear uniform.

Membership: FARC claims to represent the rural poor against the wealthier classes. Reports vary from 8000 to 30,000 members – both armed combatants and civilian supporters. 30% of the FARC guerrillas are female. Most guerrillas are younger than 19. They are not paid a wage.

Location: The rebels control approximately a third of the country (a region about the size of Switzerland), mainly in the south and east. Bases are deep inside the jungle, though FARC are active throughout Colombia on 70–80 fronts, including cells in urban areas.

Activities: Guerrilla activity against Colombian political, military and economic targets. Foreign citizens are often kidnapped for ransom or to achieve strategic aims. The extortion of legal and illegal businesses. Drugs and arms trafficking.

Weapons: Ammunition from the latest assault rifles and ground-to-air missiles, to landmines and bombs camouflaged as soccer balls and soup cans.

Funding: FARC make at least $300 million per year – up to 75% of this comes from the drugs trade.

Opponents: Governments of Colombia, the United States and Canada; the European Union; the United Nations

A photo taken by Abbot of the Nissan shortly before it became stuck in the dry riverbed.

SJ

Abbot's Journal

<u>29th Sept</u>: Pedro was right about the road. It was lousy alright — more of a pot-holed, meandering track than a road. But we met no one coming the other way, which was the key thing. The Nissan worked hard, all of its 180 bhp was needed to carve through the hanging branches and ferns. Pedro let some pressure out of the tyres to get more traction and this was needed in some boggy parts of the road. Took more than wheel traction to get us out of the steep gulley formed by a tributary of the Magdalena River. I carried the winch wire up to a tree on the other side and we used this to drag us up the slope. The ground was so boggy we nearly pulled the tree out by its roots. We reached the end of the road at sunset and made camp, ready to set off on foot tomorrow. I thought the jungle noises would keep me awake, but I feel asleep instantly.

<u>30th Sept</u>: We left the Nissan hidden in deep bush and fern cover and set up its locator transmitter. Then we set out on foot towards the tracker signal winking on my customized iPhone. We'd been cutting a path for about an hour. Jorges was in front hacking at saplings and bushes with his machete when he called out in pain. He had the head of a brown snake attached to his calf, the body of the snake he'd sliced off was still writhing on the ground. It was a bushmaster pit viper — not good. I popped open the first aid kit

and used the vacuum kit on the two fang marks, which extracted a small amount of blood but no obvious venom. There were generic antivenom ampules in the kit and I injected one of these into his calf. It was important he stayed calm to slow the path of the venom in his bloodstream. I was head of this mission, so the next decision was mine.

56

Colombia's deadly creatures

Much of Colombia is covered by thick, lush rainforest, a thriving ecosystem that is home to colourful reptiles, glossy-feathered birds, chattering insects and secretive mammals. To survive, these creatures rely on tooth, claw, stealth and venom, and for the unsuspecting traveller the rainforest can be deadly. Take bullet ants for example. These insects live in huge colonies and each ant is equipped with biting mandibles (jaws) that can cause

Bullet ant

Wandering spider –
A highly aggressive
and venomous
nocturnal hunter.
SJ

More of the supplied background information. SE operatives are required to be well informed of the flora and fauna in their active territory.

SJ

Clockwise: Mosquito; Poison dart frog; Bushmaster viper

Be wary of water too, as camouflaged crocodilians such as caimans lurk with powerful jaws filled with pointed teeth, ideal for catching and dragging prey underwater. One other deadly reptile is the bushmaster pit viper. This highly aggressive snake has extremely long fangs and any victim of its venom will suffer blood poisoning and gangrene at the very least. If antivenom is unavailable chances of survival are slim. Colombia's deadliest mammal has to be the elusive jaguar. This beautiful cat is unlikely to attack if unprovoked but a mother with cubs will fight to the death. Travellers should beware of one creature in particular, despite its minuscule size. The mosquito is responsible for thousands of deaths from malaria every year, and also transmits yellow fever and dengue fever.

excruciating pain, like a bullet ripping into the skin. And they're not alone. In the branches dwell beautiful, bright-eyed frogs. Poison dart frogs come in a myriad of colours and it is these that warn other wildlife to avoid these tiny amphibians. Toxins in their skin can kill within minutes if ingested, and they have long been used by indigenous people to smear onto spears and darts when hunting prey.

I asked Vince to help Jorges back to the jeep and get him to hospital — by helicopter if possible. Vince was not happy with this, but he knew Jorges could die without proper attention. As though on cue Jorges vomited copiously into a bush. Finally Vince agreed, through clenched teeth, but said he'd be back as soon as he could. I felt bad for him. I knew he already felt like he had let Senator Finlay down, and he didn't want to do it a second time.

An hour and a half later Pedro and I were within a mile of the source of the tracker signal. It was time to be cautious. We slithered snake-like through the undergrowth for several hundred yards and finally came across a track that had been used recently. There were fresh boot marks in the mud — military boots. We took off the safety catches on the HKs and moved down the path with rifles at shoulder height and sighted. Pedro kept rear guard as we advanced. It was just like operations in Belize — I felt taut and super-alert on the adrenalin rush.

It was midday when we saw the perimeter of the encampment through the trees. The iPod tracker light was now winking red instead of green against a satellite image of an impenetrable tree

The iPhone transmitter signal had turned red, showing Abbot was close to the source. Note that the iPhone had moved nearer to the camp.

SJ

Archive image of a FARC camp.

SJ

canopy. Our position was a distance of some 100 yards from the target. We could just make out a hut with a grass roof, so gloomy was the light under the thick covering of trees. The noise of cicadas, monkeys and birds drowned out any noise we were making as we approached.

The hut was thankfully unoccupied. Spare clothes told us it was a guard's hut and there was ammo, but no weapons. On a wooden ammo box used as a table I saw something that made my heart stand still — it was Em's iPhone, the plastic casing prised open. Someone had removed the dummy sim card, but the one built into the iPhone's circuitry had not been discovered. I pocketed the iPhone and we exited very quietly from the hut keeping rifle sights at eye-level. The dense jungle folded around us. We had to find Em — if she was still alive. And fast.

SERPENT'S EYE
SATOC

Col. D. Davies

06.10.2008
SE/DD27708

File note from Col. Davies on the discovery of Emilia Gonzalez

Abbot's journal was temporarily suspended on 30th September. I have subsequently compiled this file note from debriefs.

On 30th September, Abbot and Mori found a good position and then observed the camp through binoculars. They counted seven huts and eight guards lounging around, but saw no sign of any of the hostages.

They struck lucky late in the afternoon. They spotted a woman doing washing duties at a stream. She was barefoot and apparently without a FARC soldado guarding her. Abbot barely recognized Gonzalez – she had lost a lot of weight. But she kept her wits and did not call out when she saw them approaching, for fear of alerting a nearby guard.

Abbot and Mori explained the situation and Gonzalez quickly sketched a plan of the camp showing the location of Finlay's hut on a page of Abbot's diary. Abbot and Mori told Gonzalez that they would assess the defences and try and free her and Finlay the following day. She was to stay alert and try to warn Finlay. Gonzalez told them that she had made a sort of companion of one of the female guards, Maria Elena. Elena, it seems, was sick of the whole hostage scenario and wanted desperately to get back to her family and boyfriend.

Taking Elena into Gonzalez's confidence was a risk, but if it paid off then having someone on the inside would make it much easier to free Finlay. This was perhaps the most crucial decision that Abbot had to make, and there was little time for hesitation as a guard could check on Gonzalez at any time. Abbot asked Gonzalez if she felt that she could trust Elena. Gonzalez nodded once. Abbot accepted her decision, and they adjusted their plans to include Elena, and agreed that Elena could be told that they were planning to take her with them when they left.

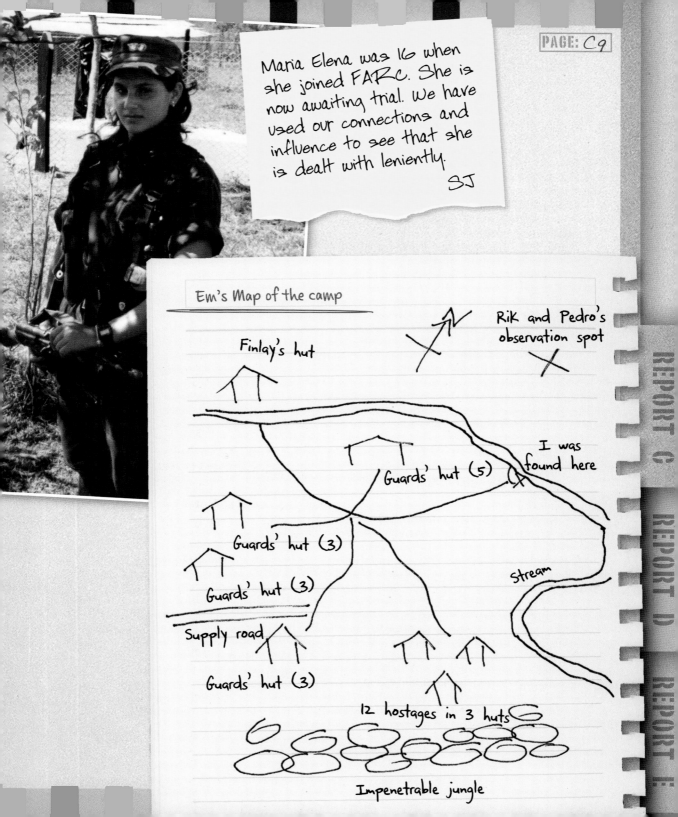

Maria Elena was 16 when she joined FARC. She is now awaiting trial. We have used our connections and influence to see that she is dealt with leniently.

SJ

Em's Map of the camp

Finlay's hut

Rik and Pedro's observation spot

Guards' hut (5)

I was found here

Guards' hut (3)

Guards' hut (3)

Stream

Supply road

Guards' hut (3)

12 hostages in 3 huts

Impenetrable jungle

REPORT C

REPORT D

REPORT E

Colombia's forgotten hostages

The daring rescue in July 2008 of Colombia's best-known hostage, French-Colombian politician Ingrid Betancourt, after six years in FARC guerrilla captivity, was a cause for celebration in Colombia and around the world. However, the Colombian press also sought to remind the world that several hundred hostages still remain in rebel hands. 'The happiness felt by all Colombians over [Ingrid's] rescue and that of her 14 colleagues is painfully countered by the pain still suffered by the families who still have not been reunited with their loved ones,' reported *El Tiempo*.

Extortion victims are under the radar

High profile political hostages such as Betancourt and Fernando Araujo Perdomo, kidnapped with the aim of furthering the agenda of the FARC and other criminal groups, are just one type of captive. The other type of prisoner are the victims of economic extortion – to which anyone is potentially vulnerable. These lower profile hostages often fall under the radar of the media outside Colombia and therefore out of the concern of the public. For instance, in the same week that Ingrid Betancourt's spectacular rescue mission made headline news around the globe, a

Fernando Araujo Perdomo, former Colombian minister of Development, escaped in 2006 after more than six years in captivity.

Norwegian-Colombian university lecturer, Alf Onshuus, was also released by the FARC after a ransom had been paid. This hardly sent a ripple through the world's media. "All the pressure from the government, from the media and from FARC is about [the] political hostages," says Olga Lucia Gomez, director of the NGO Pais Libre (Free Country). "Kidnapping a teacher is as big an aberration as kidnapping a politician." Ms Gomez warns that the official

figure of around 700 economic hostages is likely to be a substantial underestimation, as 40% of families who have had a member kidnapped for economic extortion do not report the crime to the police for fear of reprisals. However, the number of political prisoners held by the FARC is now only 28, largely because of concerted efforts by their governments such as launching rescue missions and pressuring for unilateral handovers."

27th Sept: I have been here nearly two weeks and have had no access to pen or paper until now. I am grateful to Maria Elena, who is one of my guards, for allowing me little luxuries. She is the human side of FARC. It does have one. I will try not to dwell too much on its other side. My biggest concern is that they have taken away my iPhone.

I befriended the two Australians who were taken hostage with me, but just as I was really getting to know them they were taken away. Melanie was hoping that the Australian government had brokered a deal. I hope so for their sakes.

My daily routine is like this:

6am: woken by the banging of a ladle on a cooking pot next to my ear — my signal to get the charcoal burner going to heat water for coffee and porridge. I have to make the charcoal burn with minimal smoke. The FARC are very strict about smoke.

I've put this in the file because it shows the level of hostage-taking by FARC and how unpopular it was making them. It helps to explain why Maria Elena was becoming disenchanted.

SJ

Betancourt is hailed as a heroine

3 July 2008

To the rest of the world, politician Ingrid Betancourt, 46, may have been just another one of many hostages held in the jungle by FARC. But in her native Colombia and adopted France, she is tonight being celebrated as the 'Joan of Arc of the Andes'. A steadfast campaigner against corruption, Betancourt was kidnapped while travelling into guerrilla country despite warnings. Chained by the neck for six years four months and nine days, and often tortured, she made four attempts to escape and constantly remained defiant. 'She is a great lady and a great politician who has come back to us,' said Laura Gil, a political analyst. Betancourt has called her liberation 'a miracle'.

7am: Me and two other hostages serve breakfast to the guards in the main hut. We must be respectful and quiet even when they shout at us for clumsiness or kick us to make us move out of their way. Once you learn the rules it is not so bad, but the rules vary with each guard and with their mood that day. After we have cleared away their dishes we may eat what is left over before attending other duties.

9am: Most hostages are led off to the cocina in the jungle where they collect coca leaves from the farms or work in the cocina itself. I have been given cooking and washing duties, which take all morning.

1pm: In the afternoon it is too hot for anyone to do much of anything. We lie on our straw mattresses, sleep if possible, chat, and try to keep out of the guards' way. Some days I have to do more laundry down at the stream. The women guards always want fresh clothes.

Captured photos from the FARC camp showing the guards playing football. SJ

A picture of the coca plantation managed by FARC with forced labour from hostages. SJ

5pm: It is cooler by this time and I cook the evening meal, which is usually tinned meat and kidney beans with potatoes and corn cobs from the farms.

Evening: The sun sets about 6pm and it gets dark quickly under the tree cover. We are locked up in our huts by 6.30pm. The other women talk about their families, but there is little I can say about mine. One woman sobs and prays most nights. She is very frightened.

28th Sept: I saw Finlay today as he was led to his hut. He has got very thin and looks pale and sickly. I am worried about his health and told Maria Elena as much. She said she would speak to Rosco, the camp commander, but he delights in the suffering that goes on in this place so I doubt it will come to anything.

29th Sept: Today Rosco burned my feet with his cigar again. I didn't give him the satisfaction of tears, but I couldn't help screaming each time he did it and he did it many times. He'd found some unusual features on my iPhone and wanted to know what they were. I didn't tell him. The tears come now.

Archive photos of
peasants farming coca
leaves. Finlay was put to
this back-breaking work
throughout his long ordeal.
SJ

Call made by Peron to Rizzo recorded by Softshoe. SJ

EC/DD27908
30.09.2008

Phone intercept: 30.09.08, 10:34–10:37

Rizzo: You're costing me a ███████ fortune in cell phones.

Peron: That is nothing to the fortune we'll both lose if this operation goes wrong, my friend.

Rizzo: I think you'll find there might be more than money at stake if things go wrong, MY friend.

Peron: Should I take that as a threat?

Rizzo: Take it how the hell you like. Now, give me the update for Chrissakes.

Peron: You should be more respectful, my reach is a long one. Even as far as you can go.

Rizzo: This is getting us nowhere. Let's stop the bickering shall we?

Peron: Very well. My associates are in position. They will make their visit tomorrow at 5.30 a.m. a few minutes after sunrise.

Rizzo: That's good news. What about the girl?

He means Gonzalez SJ

Peron: She is a valuable asset.

Rizzo: I think she is a risk.

Peron: You want the asset eliminated?

Rizzo: We don't need the ransom money, let's face it. Yeah. Eliminate the asset.

Peron: By this time tomorrow our little problem should have gone away. I will call you tomorrow at the same time.

Rizzo: Guess that means another ██████ cell phone.

(Conversation ends).

REPORT C   REPORT D   REPORT E

SERPENT'S EYE

SATOC

SEE TOP SECRET

REPORT D: OBJECTIVES

1. Free targets.

2. Inhibit assailants.

Battle for FARC hostages

A clash between FARC guerillas, drug smugglers' mercenaries and special forces deep in the Colombian jungle was always going to be bloody. But the human price for a US Senator held hostage was considered worth paying.

BY CHAD DERRICK

Derrick: Just set the scene for us. This was the 30th September.

Mayhew: As you know I'd gone back to Zaragoza with Ortiz. He was getting delirious and his leg was swelling up from the groin to the ankle. I radioed our Bogotá contact from the 4WD that he'd been bitten by a bushmaster snake and gave them the symptoms. They organized a chopper and medical help. By the time we reached Zaragoza the chopper was there, Ortiz was put on an IV line, given more antivenom and off he went to a specialist hospital in Bogotá. Four hours later the surgeons discovered

his leg had huge areas of gangrene. They had no other option but to amputate. Never mess with a bushmaster, man. Meanwhile I'd put together a unit of four of Mori's ex-Colombian army buddies – two of whom I'd worked with before. We set off back to where I'd last seen Abbot and Mori. I'd had a message from a source I am not at liberty to disclose, saying that there'd been an intercept.

Derrick: An intercept?

Mayhew: Let's just say that a phone conversation had been overheard. It contained some very worrying information suggesting that the camp was going to be attacked imminently and that the lives of Gonzalez and Finlay would be in the utmost danger.

Derrick: What did you decide to do?

Mayhew: It was going to be a foot race – if we got there before the attack started then we had every chance of getting the hostages out in one piece. Otherwise, they would be coming out in body bags.

We'd had radio contact with Abbot and Mori. They told us they had seen Gonzalez and that she'd told them where Finlay was held. They were planning to bust the two of them before dawn the following morning. I told Abbot to wait until we got there but I knew he had no intention of doing that.

I returned to our little jungle arsenal with my four military specialists: Eulogio Ruis, Jhon Santiago, Freddy Blanco and Diego Napa. They all had sharp-end

---

OPPOSITE : FARC soldiers armed to the teeth.
BELLOW: FARC retaliate while under attack.

experience of FARC fighting. We loaded up with RPGs, Stingers, as well as our choice of assault rifles and automatics. There would be no time for sneaking up through the undergrowth. We decided we'd have to knock on the front door, or more likely kick the damn thing down.

The other reason for speed was SL – Secrecy Leakage. You think you've kept everything tightly under wraps, but Colombia is a secrecy sieve. There are Mafia ears, FARC ears, drug dealers' ears, paramilitary ears, government ears, army ears, police ears, person-who-sells-you-enchiladas ears. The ears listen to everything and then the tongues go to work and your mission is compromised. No, speed, believe me, was of the essence.

Derrick: Do you think you were sufficiently prepared for a mission like this?

Mayhew: I did at the time. We didn't underestimate the FARC soldiers. They are ruthless. If they show cowardice then the repercussions for them are worse than death itself. But their training is basic at best and their tactical approach is haphazard. Remember, I spent six years attached to Delta Force working mostly in South America so I knew what to expect from the FARC boys and girls. Picar, though, he was different. He was as mad as a box of frogs, with a bloodlust second only to Vlad the Impaler. To answer your question, we were as well prepared as time allowed, but sufficiently prepared? I guess not.

Derrick: Describe what happened when you arrived at the camp.

Mayhew: We saw the chopper go in from a distance of about five miles from the camp. It was a Colombian Army chopper.

Derrick: What was the significance of that?

Mayhew: The Colombian Army had nothing to do with this mission. We had that from on high. This was supposed to be low profile, quick and surgical. Army capers are rarely that.

RIGHT: One of Picar's death squad approaches the FARC camp with a helicopter providing arial support.

ABOVE: Mayhew (front right) with Napa, approach the FARC camp, backed up by Ruis (far left) and Santiago.

Derrick: What about Betancourt's escape?

Mayhew: That was brilliant, but it was a one-off.

After seeing the chopper go over we were expecting the worst. Sure enough, we started to hear explosions even though we were a couple of klicks [kilometres] away. It was a whole dog's dinner of mortar shells, RPGs and automatic fire. Then we heard the unmistakable sound of 40mm grenade launchers being deployed from the chopper. That camp was getting strafed with grenades and helicopter-mounted 20mm cannon. I was not feeling optimistic about

the survival chances of those inside. Ruis confirmed aloud what I was thinking: "I don't think that's an army chopper – they don't use grenade launchers."

There was thick black smoke coming from the camp by the time we got there. I could make out the screams of injured people in the brief pauses between explosions. We took up positions at the south gate and exchanged fire with the camp guards, who seemed to be clustered across the river. I could see six or seven people down – mostly civilians. They would have been hostages or enforced labour. When you're in that situation, you have to

be hyper-focused on everything around you – snipers, grenades, tanks, helicopters, your own team, the other team, innocent civilians, trip wires… The perimeter was protected with some very nasty devices connected to trip wires. Trigger one of those babies and they flick an APG (anti personnel grenade) up above head height where it explodes, propelling a cloud of ball bearings down at supersonic speed. If you're near one, you're dead, or as good as.

Derrick: Was there any sign of Finlay or Gonzalez?

Mayhew: For what seemed like the hundredth time that day I tried

16

Abbot's radio. You'd think that with all the satellite techno magic that we had at our beck and call we'd be able to talk to each other or somehow get a message through, but hell no, there was static and nothing else. I guessed that either Abbot and Mori had busted Finlay and Gonzalez already, or they were all dead. We heard the chopper come over again and took shots at it, but we could only see it for a few seconds before it was hidden by the trees. The guys in Colombian army gear, Picar's men, were very methodical. They were working each hut quickly and ruthlessly. We took out four of them with automatic fire and may have saved some of the hostages as a result. The FARC contingent seemed to have melted away by now.

Ruis and I hot-footed it to where Picar's Land Cruisers were positioned and beat them up pretty terminally with RPGs. Those guys were not leaving in the luxury of their Toyotas at least.

We were fired on from one of the guards' huts inside the camp. That's when Ruis caught a bullet in the neck. He was 20 yards in front of me when he fell. I could see that the bullet had taken away part of his spine. He died instantly. The source of the firing came to an abrupt end as the hut exploded from an RPG fired by Blanco.

I estimated there were 14 of Picar's men on the ground, less the two we'd killed and four others who'd been killed by FARC or cross-fire. I hoped there might be some injuries among the rest, because we were down to four and Napa looked in bad shape – a piece of shrapnel

---

SERPENT'S EYE
S A T O C

article   edit this page   history

Delta Force

Also known as: Special Forces Operational Detachment-Delta, or the Combat Applications Group (CAG).

Description: An elite special operations force that's trained to the highest level in the United States Military. It is so top-secret that neither the US Government nor the US Army will confirm that Delta Force exists. Everything we know about Delta Force is unofficial.

Origin: Originally modelled on the British Special Air Service (SAS), the unit was set up by ex-SAS officer Colonel Charles Beckwith in 1977.

Aims: Counterterrorism, counterinsurgency, and national intervention operations such as eliminating covert enemy forces and rescuing hostages. Delta Force is controversial in that they undertake missions that are often on the edge of, or even breach, regular laws governing the military.

Membership: Members are recruited from all branches of the military for the special skills they possess. For instance, it is believed that Delta Force recruits must show 100% accuracy at shooting from 550 metres and 90% accuracy at 900 metres. These elite combatants are not called soldiers but operators. They wear civilian clothes and work for whoever needs them eg the army, the FBI and the CIA. In this respect, they approach the status of mercenaries. Delta Force operators are trained as professional assassins.

Organization: Delta Force is answerable only to the US President and is funded out of secret government accounts. This exposes the group to criticism that they have more power and less accountability than is morally right. Delta Force has been reported to have around 1000 operators. It is believed to be divided into three combat squadrons (A, B and C) which are composed of smaller units called troops, which can be split into small mission teams. There are squadrons for support, aviation and intelligence-gathering (reportedly the only part of the organization to include women).

Weapons: Delta Force is armed with cutting-edge weaponry – much of it having been specially customized for the unit.

search

Go   Search

navigation
- Main page
- Contents

toolbox
- What links here
- Related changes
- Upload file
- Special pages
- Printable version
- Permanent link

languages
العربية
Беларуская (тарашкевіца)
Català
Česky
Dansk
Deutsch
Español
Esperanto
Euskara
فارسی

SJ / Log out

Some updated info on Delta Force.

SJ

Some reported missions

- The 'Great Scud Hunt' during Operation Desert Storm in 1991. Delta Force operators are alleged to have infiltrated hundreds of miles into Iraq, finding Iraqi Scud missiles and killing Scud-launching crews.
- Author Mark Bowden has suggested in his book *Killing Pablo* that a Delta Force sniper might have been behind the assassination of Colombian drug lord Pablo Escobar in 1993.
- In 2003, Delta Force operators are thought to have played an important role in the invasion of Iraq. They are believed to have entered Baghdad in advance to carry out undercover missions such as: surveillance, the building of informant networks, the sabotaging of Iraqi communication lines, and the guiding of air strikes.

from an RPG had embedded itself in his right arm. Fortunately he was left-handed so he wasn't too badly affected by it.

Picar's men weren't planning to waste more time on us. Like the FARC they had disappeared into the jungle. We heard the occasional burst of fire as they shot at shadows, but they were some distance away. If I were them, I would have left a sniper positioned to at least hamper our movements, but as we dodged from hut to hut I got the feeling we weren't being watched. The camp was deserted except for the dead and injured. We injected morphine and applied field dressings where we could. My main priority was to ascertain if Finlay or Gonzalez were still in the camp, but fortunately they weren't anywhere to be seen, which most likely meant they were with Abbot and Mori.

Then as though by telepathy, my radio spoke. It was Abbot. He sounded as though he was under stress and out of breath, but he was clear and logical. He said: "We have both targets and one other."

Derrick: Finlay and Gonzalez were presumably the 'targets', but who was the 'other'?

Mayhew: She was a FARC defector called Maria Elena – and a real coup as it turned out. Abbot gave us his position and a reference point to rendezvous. He also said he was leaving a transmitter because he suspected that Picar was somehow jamming radio signals.

I told him we'd lost a man, but were otherwise alright. I saw from my map that the grid coordinate he gave me was a coded reference to a logging camp. We would be able to travel there by Land Cruiser. I was concerned that Abbot's group would make slower progress. Picar and his men would be tracking them on the ground and from the chopper. Finlay would be slowing them up if he was in bad shape, and it sounded like he was from the reports we'd had. Santiago, Blanco, Napa and I returned to the Land Cruiser without delay.

Continued on page 74.

FARC soldiers are extraordinarily well equipped for jungle fighting. Their funding largely comes from their trafficking in drugs and ransom for hostages.

SERPENT'S EYE SATOC

File note from Col. Davies

Communications have been a real problem with Abbot. I suspect that Picar has obtained some of the latest jamming equipment. We deployed some counter-measures of our own and finally made contact with Abbot on 30th September at 14.35 hours. I gave him the details of the Rizzo/Peron conversation picked up by Softshoe. It meant he had to get Gonzalez and Finlay out of the camp no later than 05.25 hours on 1st October if Picar's attack was going to be on schedule. I instructed Abbot to use the attack from Picar as a cover for his own activities – make the two things overlap if possible to confuse the FARC.

He has C4 explosives, some RPGs, flash-bang grenades and now we have re-established communications we can do what we can to direct him out of trouble. Satellite photography is rendered pretty useless by the tree cover, but we can use thermal imaging to detect the movement of people. He has brains and courage, but what he is really going to need is luck.

article | edit this page | history

Thermal imaging

Infrared Thermography (thermal imaging) is a type of infrared imaging science in which thermographic cameras detect radiation and produce images of that radiation. Infrared radiation is a type of radiation emitted by objects based on their temperatures.

Search

ion
n page
ntents

at links here
lated changes
load file
ecial pages
intable version
rmanent link

ages
بار
anapyская
арашкевіца)
atalà
esky
ansk
eutsch
spañol
speranto
uskara
فارسی

When viewed by thermographic camera, warm objects stand out against cooler backgrounds. Humans and other warm-blooded animals become visible against the environment, day or night. Because of this, thermography is of particular use to the military and security services whenever they need night vision.

Uses of thermography

Thermal imaging has many uses. Firefighters use it to find people in thick smoke and locate the heart of a blaze. In industry, technicians use thermal imaging to locate overheating machinery parts or identify heat leaks, to prevent ruptures or explosions of equipment. Thermal imaging cameras are installed in some cars as a safety feature for night driving, the first being the 2000 Cadillac DeVille.

Apparently the female FARC soldiers were very particular about their appearance. Maria Elena photographed here having her hair braided.

SJ

Gonzalez's Diary

1st Oct: Looking back over the last few days I find it hard to believe what has happened. I know that I was trained for situations like this, but until you are faced with the realities of death and cruelty, you cannot ever imagine the sadness and stupidity of it all. There were times in that camp when I was convinced I would be there forever, but as soon as I saw Rik down by the stream I knew somehow that we would get out. He has a quiet power that you can just put utter faith in. I needed some faith after what the FARC had put me through.

And I put my faith in Maria Elena — a huge gamble. Her eyes shone with pleasure when I told her we would take her with us, but we needed her help. She needed to make sure we had shoes and that our huts would be unlocked by 5am. She promised me she would do everything she could and I knew she meant it.

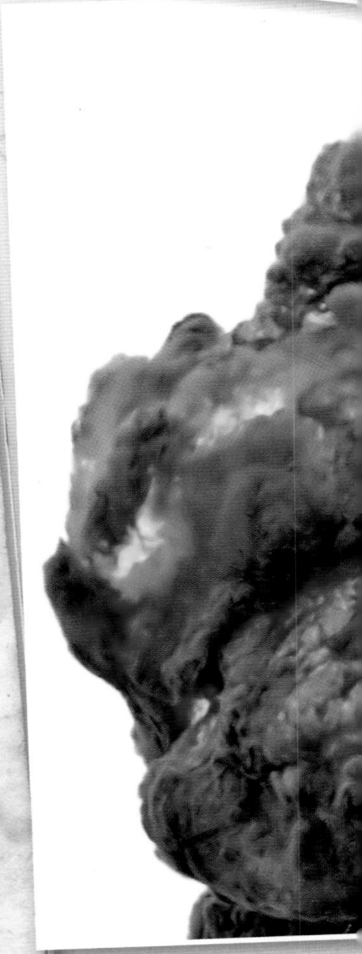

Our escape was simplicity itself. Although the FARC take heavy precautions about some things, they can also be quite dumb. The road into the camp was fortified with trip wires, APGs, sniper posts, you name it. If there was to be any attack they figured it would be from that road or by air. The one thing they did not expect was for two guys to come at them from the forest. During last night Rik and Pedro planted explosives just outside the perimeter fence on the access road. These were timed to go off at 5.13am. Duffy had passed Rik information from an intercepted telephone conversation that Picar's attack was timed for 5.30am. That gave us 17 minutes to get to Finlay and get into the cover of the jungle. I'd managed to speak with Finlay after I deliberately dropped a tray of food by him in the cantina last night. As he helped me pick up the mess I whispered to him about the plans. He was worried that he was in no fit state to make an escape bid. I told him that it might be his only chance. He said that if anything happened to him I must go to an address in Bogota where I'd find the evidence he was gathering. That was all we had time for.

Venga – Spanish meaning 'come on' SJ

2nd Oct: Just after the first hint of dawn yesterday, the sky was lit up to the south, followed by a huge blast. This was Rik's timed C4 charges detonating down by the first outpost. FARC militia poured out of their huts, pulling on boots and shouting, 'Venga, venga.' Four of them rushed into a Land Cruiser and tore off down the dirt track that was the only vehicle access into the camp, but they didn't get far because they hit one of the land mines Rik and Pedro had placed a few hours before. I heard the explosion and then saw the flames and smoke above the trees. Pedro used some C4 to blow open the security cage around Finlay's hut while Rik came to my hut and gave me a Glock pistol and some rounds of ammunition, plus combat clothes to

change into. Maria Elena appeared in full combat gear and with an assault rifle. We hugged each other briefly – how bizarre, guard and prisoner hugging each other! We had to move fast before the guards realized what was happening. I passed a body, its legs trussed up with the balls and twine of a bolas, a look of terror frozen on its bloated face. I realized with a mixture of feelings that it was Rosco.

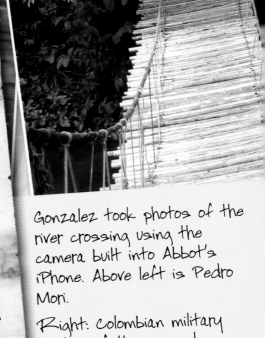

RiK said he'd been garrotted. The five of us crossed the stream, went past the perimeter hut, and followed the path that RiK and Pedro had taken on their way to the camp. We hit the dirt at a hand motion from RiK as a helicopter flew over above us. We heard the crackle of a Gatling gun and the whoosh of rockets fired into the camp. I could only think of the other hostages. They can't have stood a chance. But this was the diversion we needed to make some distance from the camp.

We reached a rope bridge and filed across it. At the other side Pedro used his hunting Knife to cut through the ropes and the bridge fell into the rushing waters with a clatter of wooden poles. He took lengths of the supporting rope and coiled them around his chest.

We then had a steep climb through thick undergrowth which took a good hour, during which time we had to fall flat on our faces several times as the helicopter

Gonzalez took photos of the river crossing using the camera built into Abbot's iPhone. Above left is Pedro Mori.

Right: Colombian military photos of the second crossing further upstream used by Picar's men.

SJ

returned. Rik had told me all about Picar by then — I knew we were dealing with someone who was far more ruthless than the FARC — even Rosco. Rik asked me if I was ok and why was I limping. I said I was ok, but he insisted I took off my shoes and socks. He looked at the soles of my feet, where Rosco's cigars had burned and blistered the skin while my feet were held in wooden stocks. He looked intently into my eyes and the world seemed to stop for a moment. Rik eventually made radio contact with Mayhew and gave him a map ref for a logging camp — our rendezvous.

REPORT D REPORT E

iPhone photos of the descent from the escarpment using ropes from the rope bridge.

If we thought the climb was bad, we were totally unprepared for the descent on the other side. For a mile or more we had climbed a rocky escarpment covered in trees and ferns. (Finlay was amazing. Not strength — he had none — but pure guts got him up that incline and he earned all our respect). We could see half a mile away a clearing and drifting smoke. It was clearly the illegal logging operation. Below we were faced with a sheer drop of about 100 feet into a tree canopy. We had to get down this or go back down the hill we'd just climbed and meet who knows what coming the other way. At certain points there were tree roots hanging over the rock. Whether they reached to the ground we couldn't tell, but they felt firm and strong. We abseiled down into the canopy using the ropes from the bridge. We were all badly scratched by thorns and eaten alive by tree ants, but we all made it to the ground.

F.I.R.E. (Forensic Incident Reconstructi

Location: Zaragoza Ridge

Date: 01.09.08

Summary: Reconstruction showing the rope bridge demolished by SE, the climb through jungle to the ridge, the abseil route through the canopy and the site of the logging camp.

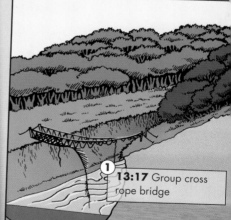

1 **13:17** Group cross rope bridge

Training manual illustration made by Van Dyke from Abbot's sketches of the ascent to the ridge and the abseil into the jungle below.
SJ

SEE

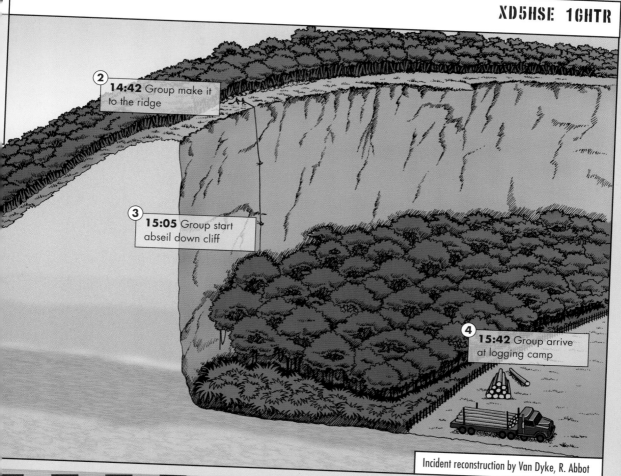

Approaching the logging camp from the escarpment. SJ

Mori covered the team with his HK33 on the way to the logging camp. SJ

XD5HSE 1GHTR

2 **14:42** Group make it to the ridge

3 **15:05** Group start abseil down cliff

4 **15:42** Group arrive at logging camp

Incident reconstruction by Van Dyke, R. Abbot

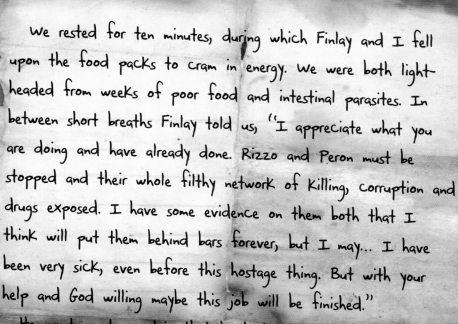

We rested for ten minutes, during which Finlay and I fell upon the food packs to cram in energy. We were both light-headed from weeks of poor food and intestinal parasites. In between short breaths Finlay told us, "I appreciate what you are doing and have already done. Rizzo and Peron must be stopped and their whole filthy network of killing, corruption and drugs exposed. I have some evidence on them both that I think will put them behind bars forever, but I may... I have been very sick, even before this hostage thing. But with your help and God willing maybe this job will be finished."

He went on to explain that he had cancer. For seven months it had been left untreated while he was in the FARC camp and his prospects were not good. He gave us details of his own apartment in Bogota but said we needed to search Rizzo's home on Martha's Vineyard for the final damning piece of the puzzle.

We macheted our way through thick undergrowth, moving in the direction of the logging camp. Rik kept checking our position on his adapted iPhone and had confirmation from Duffy that we had about 20 minutes advantage over Picar and his mercenaries.

The hill the logging truck came down as it was confronted with the helicopter.
SJ

Continued from page 18.

Picar's comms-jamming trickery seemed to have failed so I was able to keep in radio contact with Abbot as we made our way to the reference point. Yet again we arrived as a fire-fight was going on. As we entered the clearing I could make out Mori and Finlay crouched beside a pile of logs. It looked as though Mori and Maria Elena were giving covering fire to Gonzalez and Abbot who were making for a logging truck. Automatic and shot gun rounds were coming from a tin hut.

We all jumped out of the Land Cruiser and made for cover behind the huge tree trunks lying everywhere and directed shots at the hut. Abbot climbed up into the truck cab followed by Gonzalez and started the engine. I saw a puff of dust kick up next to Mori and then another. I shouted to them, "Stay down, stay down!" These were sniper shots coming from a high ridge about half a mile away – it had to be Picar. I set my rifle up on its tripod and rapid fired at where I guessed the sniper was hidden – it might have saved a few seconds. The huge logging truck with Abbot at the wheel pulled up next to Mori and Finlay, barring the sniper's view of them. My boys gave intensified fire into the hut, which then went quiet. By now Finlay, Mori and the FARC girl were inside the cab in the back compartment and the truck was moving again towards the site entrance. It was a one-in-a-million, no billion, shot. As the truck left the cover of the log pile a sniper's bullet caught Finlay in the head and killed him instantly...

Mayhew, this big tough Texan, afraid of nothing and no one, needed a few minutes to recover himself. He stared into the middle distance while his eyes moistened a little and then continued his story.

The logging camp where the fighting took place between illegal loggers and the escaping hostages. These photos were taken by Colombian forces two days after the incident.

Mayhew: He was a friend as well as my boss you know. He had an inborn sense of justice and he was not afraid to see justice done no matter what dangers it could mean for him. Yeah, I knew about his cancer. It was prostate cancer and it probably wouldn't have killed him if he'd been allowed the proper drugs an' all. I guess he would have preferred the quick death, but that didn't stop me being as angry as hell and bent on delivering my own form of justice.

Derrick: What happened after Finlay was shot?

Abbot put his foot down and roared out of the logging camp while we fell in behind in the Land Cruiser. There were no more shots from the loggers, but there was rapid shooting from the ridge. Bullets were ricocheting everywhere, but then the road turned a corner and we were sheltered by trees again. There was one thing that could stop us now – I knew it and Abbot knew it.

ABOVE: After the escape, the logging truck was found abandoned in the jungle.

Derrick: And what was that?

Mayhew: The helicopter. It had been absent for the last hour. Possibly it had gone back for refuelling and more ammo.

We were headed down a steep track, maybe a 1 in 6 gradient. Abbot was fighting to control the logging truck, but doing a fine job. Then the chopper slid into view from behind the tree line, hovering 50 feet above the road. There was a burst from the Gatlings and wood chips scythed everywhere from the truck's load. Then a Stinger missile flew from the cab of the truck and snaked towards the helicopter, exploding on contact and blowing the chopper to kingdom come. I discovered later that Gonzalez had blown out the truck's windows with her Glock, levelled the Stinger on the dashboard and fired at the helicopter all in one seamless action. That girl is something else.

Next issue: In the third part of this exclusive interview Chad Derrick discovers the fate of the Coke Father, Estafan Peron. ■

Deforestation in Colombia

Colombia contains some of the world's most spectacular forests. In fact, forest makes up 58.5% (60,728,000 hectares) of Colombia's land mass and of this 87.4% is classified as primary forest, the most biodiverse form of forest.

According to figures from the World Conservation Monitoring Centre, Colombia has some 3429 known species of amphibians, birds, mammals and reptiles. Of these, about 18% are endemic, meaning that they exist in no other country, and 10% are threatened species. Colombia is home to at least 51,220 species of vascular plants, of which nearly 30% are endemic.

However, unfortunately, deforestation over the past 30 years has been enormous. Some experts estimate that 200,000 hectares are now deforested each year, although others calculate that the figure is nearer 300,000 hectares, due to illegal deforesting activities. One of the main causes of deforestation is a government policy called the Plan Pacifico, part of ambitious plans to develop Colombia's economy. The Plan has sought since the mid-1980s to exploit the rich natural resources of the Pacific coastal rainforests. Logging has been actively encouraged, to increase the manufacturing of wood and paper; illegal logging is also widespread, and extremely difficult to track down and prevent. Huge areas of forest have also been cleared for the laying of African palm plantations as a cash crop for export. According to one estimate, in the mid-1990s, industrial gold mining alone cleared 80,000 hectares of forest per year. And as a result of this uncontrolled mining, siltation and mercury

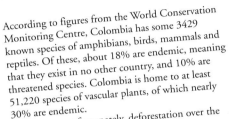

contaminated rivers, leading to a decrease in mangrove coverage. The installation of commercial shrimp farms has also resulted in the deforestation of mangrove swamps. Furthermore, in order to promote trade, Plan Pacifico attempts to link a 54 km missing section of the Pan-American Highway between Colombia and Panama; the resulting road construction and rapid regional development will have a massive impact on deforestation.

Around 100,000 hectares per year are also deforested illegally to grow coca, marijuana and opium poppies, and to set up the processing plants necessary to turn these into drugs for the streets. Colombia is a leading producer of coca, much of which is grown by very poor farmers because it generates more income than any other crop. Government efforts to clamp down on the drugs trade have involved aerial fumigation programmes where potently toxic herbicides are dropped by crop-duster planes on suspected coca plantations. However, the herbicides of course destroy not just the illegal crops but all the surrounding vegetation too. Moreover, the poverty-stricken farmers who are reliant on farming coca for their livelihood have started to move into more remote regions in order to escape the government's coca eradication efforts. The farmers are clearing new areas of forest to plant

their coca seedlings, while also hu... wildlife for food. Despite the Colo... government spending billions of d... halt the coca farmers, since the mi... of land farmed for coca has in fact ...

This deforestation does not just have devastating effects on the environment. The forests are also home to Colombia's indigenous peoples, who live off the land by sustainable means. Deforestation has begun to erode these communities' century-old ways of life. The human intrusion inflicted on these peoples by deforestation has also resulted in increased crime, alcoholism, domestic violence and

... (as many indigenous peoples are forced to abandon their ancient customs and move elsewhere).

Some expert observers have estimated that at this rate of deforestation, Colombia's forests will be depleted in just 40 years. Determined action needs to take place immediately if one of the most beautiful regions on earth is not to be destroyed forever.

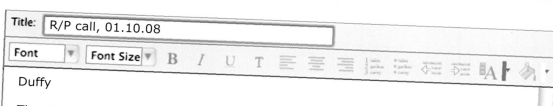

Title: R/P call, 01.10.08

Font ▼ Font Size ▼ **B** *I* <u>U</u> T

Duffy

That Mont Blanc fountain pen is earning its keep. Here is a transcript of the latest phone call between our two friends Peron and Rizzo. Sounds as though all is not sweetness and light between them.

Softshoe

SE/DD31508

Phone intercept: 01.10.08, 19:42–19:44

> Rizzo is referring to the polls favouring Obama in the forthcoming US Presidential election.   SJ

Peron: I have good news.

Rizzo: You mean the opinion polls have it all wrong?

Peron: It seems my associates have been effective. Our main problem has been removed.

Rizzo: Excellent.

Peron: And some not so good news.

Rizzo: I'm still listening.

Peron: The 'asset' – seems the asset was greater than we thought. She – it – caused a few problems.

Rizzo: And what are you doing about it?

Peron: This is not my problem, my friend. It's our problem. You, like me, will see that all loose ends are tied up. Any leads, any papers, any evidence, you and I will see that everything is destroyed. We are dealing with some unknown elements. I suggest you start right away.

Rizzo: Yet again I hear a threat. Let me tell you something. My sources tell me that your latest shipment was a foul up. There is a trace back to your factory. I would start clearing your stables of manure if I were in your riding boots.

Peron: You will not be hearing from me again my friend, but I promise you this is not the end of our business together.

(Conversation ends with much foul language from Rizzo).

> Rizzo is referring to the seizure of the narco sub and its cargo of cocaine. SJ

SERPENT'S EYE

SATOC

SEE TOP SECRET

REPORT E: OBJECTIVES

1. Retrieve evidence.

2. Pursue suspects through all available legal channels.

SUCCESSES IN THE 'WAR ON DRUGS'

An anti-drugs patrol in Colombia in 2008.

The United States has been leading the international community in waging a 'war on drugs' since President Nixon first used the term in 1971.

One thrust is to combat drug abuse and trafficking on the streets, as President Bill Clinton urged in April 1993: "We have to do a better job of preventing drug use and treating those who seek treatment and we must do more to protect law-abiding citizens from those who victimize them in the pursuit of drugs or profit from drugs." However, the support of countries where the drugs are produced is even more crucial.

Colombian President Alvaro Uribe has invested more than $4 billion on ridding his country of the drug trade. As a result, drug seizures have been increasing. In 2005, 168.5 tonnes of cocaine were seized by Colombian authorities, the largest total amount for six years. And according to the Colombian Anti-Narcotics Police and the Colombian Drugs Observatory, "In 2006, eradication work in Colombia prevented 1643 tonnes of cocaine from reaching the streets of the world and $41.073 billion from reaching drug traffickers."

Some recent single drugs seizures have been on a

SEE TOP SECRET

File note from Col. Davies to SATOC executive

During the last six years, $4.7 bn of US funds have gone into coca eradication schemes. Much of this money was not used to destroy coca farms and factories, nor to establish compensation packages for the displaced coca farmers. Instead it was syphoned off by drugs barons such as Estafan Peron with the collusion of a certain corrupt US government official, namely Senator David Rizzo, who was partially responsible for the distribution of these funds. The huge sums of money were then laundered. This involved New York based Mafia organizations expert in handling unwieldy supplies of illicit money.

SATOC, in conjunction with the US and Colombian governments, has agreed upon a very specific and focused attack on the coca farms identified as those of Peron. In parallel with this action, Serpent's Eye Operatives will seek to secure evidence collected by and identified by the late Senator Nick Finlay, whose sad death this organization deeply regrets. His death will not have been in vain if the perpetrators of the destructive and vile trade in drugs are dealt a serious blow.

Colonel Davies

spectacular scale. In 2007, almost 13 tonnes of cocaine was found ready for export in a hide on the Pacific Coast. The drugs belonged to various trafficking organizations and the haul was the result of eight months of undercover work by Colombia's secret intelligence service. While in 2008, after a six-month intelligence operation, Colombian authorities discovered more than ten tonnes of cocaine worth $200 million in the Caribbean city of Barranquilla, ready to be shipped to Mexico. The drugs were hidden among boxes of children's toys and belonged to 'Madman Barerra' – one of the two most powerful drug traffickers in the country.

Also in 2008, one of the most wanted Colombian cocaine barons, Edgar Vallejo-Guarin, was arrested in Spain. Accused of heading one of Colombia's biggest and most violent cocaine cartels, and of moving many millions of dollars worth of the drug into the US, Western Europe and Britain, Vallejo-Guarin had been wanted by a US Federal Court in Florida since 2001 on multiple charges. There was a $5 million price on his head. Eduardo Aguirre, the US ambassador to Spain, described the drug baron's capture as an excellent example of international cooperation in the war against drug trafficking.

Email from Col. Davies to SATOC executive SJ

Title: Joint US/Colombian Special Forces op

Font | Font Size | **B** *I* U T

Further to the last communication No. SE/2860, I can confirm that a joint US/Colombian Special Forces op was staged last night. As you know this has been some months in preparation, but we had to have conclusive evidence before executing the plan or the political fall-out would have been damaging for all concerned. The timing was crucial. We gave the special unit the confirmation of the date for the action the moment we knew Finlay had been killed and that Peron and Rizzo were implicated. We had to move before Finlay's evidence had been destroyed. The outcome of the action was totally satisfactory. Attached is an inventory of Peron's confiscated property etc. Please note I will be in transit to New York after sending this.

SERPENT'S EYE
SATOC

Col. D. Davies

02.10.2008

SE/2861/B

Inventory of Peron's confiscated property

- Hacienda south of Caucasia in North-West Colombia; a ranch near Zaragoza; a luxury apartment in Bogotá; a luxury villa by the sea outside Cartagena; a penthouse overlooking Central Park, NY; a $55m luxury yacht moored at Cartagena. Estimated property worth $230m.

- Approximately 20 tonnes of cocaine ready for shipment. Estimated wholesale value $50m.

- Cocaine destroyed at Peron's cocinas, awaiting purification – very approximate value: $20m.

- Cash at hacienda, Peron's bribery funds: $7m.

- Frozen funds at banks (we are working with lawyers to extract this): $130m.

Peron was defiant during his capture SJ

Hasta la vista

They came out of a clear blue sky with no warning. Four attack helicopters bearing crack troops of a combined US and Colombian force with one thing on their minds: destroy the cocaine farms and get the one named the Coke Father, Estafan Peron. In this third part of his VORTEX interview with one-time body guard to Senator Nick Finlay, Chad Derrick discovers what happened on the fateful day of 1st October 2008.

his was the third and last day of my extensive interview with Vince Mayhew, conducted in a remote Nebraskan farmhouse. Mayhew was less tense than on the first day. Perhaps he truly believed he could trust me by then. We drank home-made cappuccinos and ate bagels from the freezer. Mayhew, an ex-smoker, jiggled some dog tags in his big, scar-laced hand.

Derrick: What happened after Finlay was killed?

Mayhew: We decided to go for Peron without delay. The operation for taking him had been meticulously planned for months between Colombian and US special forces.

Derrick: How did you get involved in these plans?

Mayhew: Finlay had a lot of good friends in high office. When he was killed some of

ABOVE: Estafan Peron is escorted away from the hacienda by Colombian security forces.

Peron's fortified hacienda near Caucasia in North-West Colombia.

precious informer whose family had suffered at Peron's hands. And there was concentrated satellite surveillance on his hacienda plus on-the-ground surveillance. We knew his weapons manifest, his tactics, his getaway plans and his minute-to-minute whereabouts.

There is a bit of technology that is rather useful. You probably know that the blast of a nuclear bomb kills all radio signals with a huge electromagnetic pulse [EMP]. Well, it's possible to create an EMP without setting off a nuclear bomb. Without going into details, we knocked out Peron's communications, making him as blind and deaf as a newborn mouse. That's when we hit him. Four Black Hawks came in while his drones were going hoopla over their blank security monitors, their dead radios, their snuffed computers and even their silent cell phones. We created a lot of noise with flash-bangs, took out a few guards, blew up his getaway chopper and fleet of luxury Land Rangers with a deal of C4.

Derrick: And what of Peron?

Mayhew: He'd gone underground, literally. All that money buys a lot of security, but not much good if you have no coms. We blasted into his personal inner sanctum and found a spiral staircase going deep underground. It went down to a bombproof bunker, but by then we had some of his guards and techno guys. Boy did they hate his guts. When they realized there was to be no escape for Peron they fell over themselves to give us the codes to the locks securing his bunker.

When Peron realized the game was up he surrendered surprisingly quickly. You know why?

Derrick: No, why?

Mayhew: Because he believed that with his power and money and influence, if we got him by a miracle

those friends felt that his ex-bodyguard might have a special commitment to dealing with his assassins.

Derrick: It was personal then?

Mayhew: You can say that again. I had also led operations like this before, I knew the territory, and I knew something about Peron and

his pet psychopath, Picar. So, I went straight from Zaragoza to Barrancabermeja where the assault team was assembled.

Peron had a fortified hacienda south of Caucasia. Ever since the *Leviathan* incident when the narc sub was taken off Carlsbad, Peron's card had been marked. We had a

RIGHT: Colombian security forces burn the cocinas where Peron's coca farmers manufactured cocaine.

out of the hacienda, then he'd be freed by the end of the day. And should he in some parallel world be made to stand trial, then he'd fix a judge so that he would be free within a month. And should there be some incredible sequence of mishaps and he was jailed, then after a few months of inconvenience, he would be free. His farms would still be there, the money would still be rolling in.

Derrick: Why are you laughing?

Mayhew: Oh it was good to see his world gradually disintegrate after getting a glimpse of all the thousands of worlds he'd made fall apart. It made everything worthwhile. Finlay would have enjoyed himself. No, we didn't plan for Señor Peron to be back in business within a year or within a forever. And after we'd taken him to a very, very secure jail in Bogotá we showed him live video coverage of his coca farms being incinerated and his coke cocinas being blown to hell. We showed him his coke stores in San Antero, ready for shipment, being raided and the coke being loaded on to US Navy vessels. There was over 20 tonnes of the stuff. I just hope he is not too comfortable doing his life sentence in La Picota jail.

Derrick: What about Picar?

Mayhew: One thing did not go quite to plan. Picar has a sixth, seventh and eighth sense. He should have been at the hacienda that day, but he'd already taken a flight on one of his many passports. Destination – at that point in time – unknown.

Continued on page 62.

First noticed when testing nuclear bombs in the 1950s, the electromagnetic pulse created by the blast fried all surrounding circuitry. Since then the military have been trying to harness this powerful technology. Mayhew is referring to something called an EMP Magnifier – basically a flux generator connected to an antenna. A controlled explosion shoots a metal core through an electric coil releasing a terawatt of microwave pulses and knocking out all electronic components in its wake. SJ

REPORT E

Abbot's Journal

3rd Oct: Em needed medical treatment for the open sores on her feet, courtesy of Rosco's cigars. She really needed complete rest, but she had enough spirit to run an army truck. And Finlay had entrusted her with the details of his Bogota cache of evidence against Rizzo. We drove through the night to Finlay's apartment in Bogota arriving at 03.26 hours yesterday. The street was lit by one feeble lamp. A dog was barking somewhere. We were three: Em, Pedro and myself. Maria Elena was being held for questioning in Barrancabermeja. Vince was on a specials' op to get Peron.

Finlay's apartment was on the first floor. Vince had given us keys. The apartment was the kind of style that a bachelor like Finlay would choose to rent. Clean, unfussy lines, abstract art on the walls, minimal but comfortable furnishings, everything neat as a pin. The only odd thing was that a modern painting by a popular Colombian artist was upside down. I would never have known, but Em noticed at once. She took the painting off its hook, revealing a safe in the wall underneath. It was unlocked and completely empty. Em looked at me with tears in her eyes. "I can't believe it. We were the only ones who knew about this, weren't we?" She looked at Pedro, who shook his head in reply, looking grim. "You can keep very few secrets from a man of Peron's wealth."

I went into the bedroom and phoned Duffy.

They found the safe behind a print of a painting by a contemporary Colombian artist. SJ

03.10.2008

SE/SJ32708

E9

Transcript of phone conversation between Abbot and Col. Davies: 02.10.2008, 10:33

Abbot: We are at Finlay's rented apartment in Bogotá. I'm afraid someone has been here before us. The safe is empty.

Col. Davies: Let's think a moment. Now we've got Peron where we want him, he might just help nail Rizzo. According to Softshoe there's no love lost between those two. Softshoe is going with Rizzo tomorrow to his summer house on Martha's Vineyard. She's very resourceful, but she may need help.

Abbot: You want us to go there Duffy?

Col. Davies: Hold on a sec. (Silence lasting 26 seconds) Right. There's a flight from Bogotá to JFK at 08:00 hours. I'll book four tickets – Mayhew will be joining you. I'll also make arrangements to get you to Martha's Vineyard by tomorrow evening. Get some sleep on the plane. All of you.

(Conversation ends).

Martha's Vineyard

article | edit this page | history

Martha's Vineyard is an island off the United States' east coast, to the south of Cape Cod, in the state of Massachusetts. At 32 kilometres long, it is the 57th largest island in the US and adjoins the smaller Chappaquiddick Island. Chappaquiddick was where, in 1969, the dead body of Mary Jo Kopechne was found in the submerged car of Senator Edward Kennedy, a scandal that put the islands on the map. Subsequently, the filming of the blockbuster movie *Jaws* in 1975 brought visitors flocking to the island – which is accessible only by ferry and air. Martha's Vineyard became popular as the perfect destination to spend the summer, and soon movie stars, politicians, artists and celebrities had all bought vacation properties there. A visit by the Clintons in the 1990s made Martha's Vineyard even more desirable and today the cost of living and of property on the island is considerably higher than the national average. The island is low key and quiet – a haven for famous affluent people who go there to enjoy the natural beauty and the laidback atmosphere, not to be seen.

REPORT

Col. D. Davies
SE/DD32908

03.10.2008

File note from Col. Davies

Someone got to Finlay's safe in his Bogotá apartment before our crew did. The most likely suspect is Picar. He found out how much Rosco knew and then made certain Rosco was killed in the attack on the camp. It is likely that Finlay was drugged and tortured for information during the seven months he spent in the FARC camps. He may have thought his secret was still safe, but seven months of what he went through would be enough to remove secrets from anyone.

We have another piece of gadgetry that sounds as though it came from the fertile imagination of James Bond's Q rather than a rather boring but masterly hacker known to us as Van Dyke. The EMP Magnifier used to disrupt Peron's communications at his hacienda was an unqualified success, and we are thankful to the US Government for its loan to us. But for the RHDC (Remote Hard Drive Cloner), we must thank our very own Mr Van Dyke. It looks like a simple but over-large flash drive, it fits into any USB port or works remotely like a router, has 160 Gigs of space and it duplicates the entire hard drive of the computer into which it is plugged or tuned – no matter what firewalls or anti-virus software is installed, Van Dyke's gizmo waltzes around them and faithfully copies every password, and every document on the unwitting computer.

Softshoe suspects from a conversation overheard between Rizzo and one of his aides, that the computer at his summer house on Martha's Vineyard is the main archive. She thinks it may contain evidence of the misappropriation of US funds for coca eradication programmes, as well as evidence that Rizzo holds against Peron and New York Mafia organizations. She has got to know him quite well. He is ruthless but organized. He stores facts and evidence for a rainy day when he might need to put someone behind bars or have them taken out. With Peron in custody and awaiting trial, he is jumpy. Softshoe needs to clone his computer on Martha's Vineyard and she has no time to lose.

Meanwhile I have sent Abbot, Gonzalez, Mori and Mayhew to Rosemount – Softshoe may need some help.

RHDC – Remote Hard Drive Cloner

SATOC INFOBASE
FILE: 874V

The Remote Hard Drive Cloner is one of the computer industry's best kept secrets. The RHDC contains constantly updating software to enable it to get past all firewall protection and clone files from a target computer's hard drive.

Slightly larger than a flash drive, the RHDC can work from a USB port or remotely via a wireless signal.

1. USB connector
2. Main processing unit
3. Network finder
4. Digital display
5. Memory compression/storage
6. Log-in light

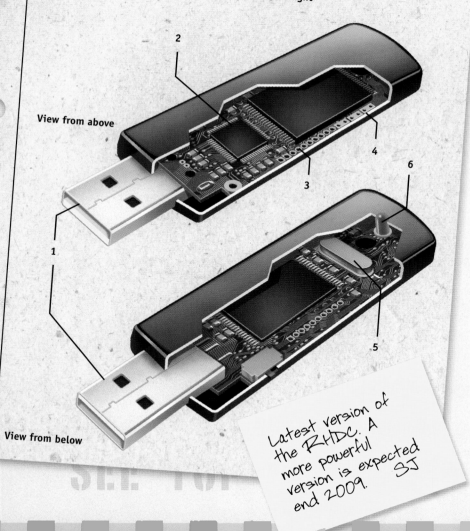

View from above

View from below

Latest version of the RHDC. A more powerful version is expected end 2009.   SJ

We have this conversation thanks to the voice activated-recorder/transmitter fountain pen in Rizzo's possession.

SJ

SE/EC33708
03.10.2008

1/2

Transcript of conversation between Softshoe (Campbell) and Rizzo: 03.10.08

Campbell: Judging by the size of this pad, not to mention the original Remingtons on the walls, it would seem the credit crunch hasn't really squeezed you too hard, sweetie.

Rizzo: Credit crunch? What credit crunch? I thought you'd realize that I don't need to borrow money. I'm the one who lends it to suckers who can't get it any other way.

Campbell: At high rates of interest, naturally.

Rizzo: Naturally.

Campbell: You're a loan shark then. What happens if your borrowers don't pay up? I assume you don't send them a firm but fair letter like the one I get from my bank manager when I go over my limit?

Rizzo: They always pay up. One way or another. Anyway, I don't lend to those poor shmucks who can't pay their mortgages because the price of gas has gone up a few cents. We are talking bigger deals — the kind your average bank tends not to be very keen on. People who suffered because of the credit crunch are just bad planners. They deserve whatever they get.

Campbell: That's not exactly what you've been saying in your election speeches, Senator Rizzo.

Rizzo: Election? You call this fiasco an election? The media has been rigged against us from day one, the funds are locked up in the bank crisis and the scumbles in the opposition are telling lies like they were on special discount.

SE/EC33708
03.10.2008

2/2

(At this point Rizzo produced a gun from his desk drawer).

> Talking of fiascos, I think it's time this little charade was over. I don't know who you are working for or exactly what you know about my business interests, but in two hours a rather frightening individual called Juan Picar will arrive here and he will, let's say, 'interview' you. He is looking forward to meeting you. I've given you quite a write-up.

Campbell: Why do you say he's 'frightening', David?

Rizzo: I would prefer you not to find out why. I have quite enjoyed your company these last few weeks. I don't especially want you to be slowly and agonizingly tortured to death by Picar. So tell me what you know and Picar can be denied his pleasures with you.

Campbell: It's very simple – and please put that silly gun away darling. I am a journalist. I wanted to get close to a senator who was close to the action before the change in government. It makes a good celebrity feature. I admit it was a little devious of me. But nothing terrible, believe me. I won't write it if this is how you feel darling. Honestly.

Rizzo: You're right, you won't be writing it. And especially not with this.

(Rizzo took the Mont Blanc pen from his pocket, the one he had stolen from her, tossed it to her and tutted).

> Very stupid of you. What you may have heard on this little toy is going to cost you dearly. I suggest you start unburdening yourself before Picar turns up. He could be early. Tell me what you know 'darling' and I promise to get you out of Picar's way.

(Conversation ends).

Derrick: You said that Finlay's safe had been emptied in his Bogotá apartment. What were your options now?

Mayhew: Limited. Finlay had sworn affidavits in that safe from coca farmers who had been forced to sign papers saying they had received funds from the US government to stop coca farming. They never saw any of the money, of course. He also had signed papers from Rizzo confirming these same farmers had received funds and that he had visited them personally. It wasn't cast-iron proof, but it was enough to indict Rizzo and that fact alone could make Peron start his plea bargaining and squealing on Rizzo – Peron was in denial. He simply could not understand that his money was not opening doors, especially his cell door.

Without going into details, an associate had managed to infiltrate Rizzo's nasty little world. She had even more evidence than Finlay had managed to gather, but she was in some danger.

Derrick: In what way?

Mayhew: She was at Rizzo's mansion on Martha's Vineyard with Rizzo, which was dangerous enough, but we had reason to believe that Picar had been behind the safe robbery and that he had taken a flight to New York. We thought he was looking for Rizzo on Peron's orders. There was always the chance of collateral damage with Picar.

So we took a flight to New York and all slept like dead dogs the whole way. At JFK we transferred to a Learjet. We were met on board by a Brit who was only ever referred to as Mr Briscoe. I assumed he was MI6 or SIS but it was not my business to ask. The others seemed to respect him highly and that was good enough for me. We touched

An artist's impression of Rizzo's summer house, Rosemount, on Martha's Vineyard.

down at Martha's Vineyard Airport just 45 minutes later armed, courtesy of Mr Briscoe, with an array of weaponry all of which seemed familiar to the others.

By the time we'd driven to Rosemount, Rizzo's summer house near Harthaven, it was dark, but there was a full moon. The house was deep inside a wood so we could approach on foot to within 300 yards without being seen. Compared to Peron's hacienda we knew it was relatively unprotected, though encircled by a high fence and watched over by security

cameras and Rizzo's retinue of two muscle men. Abbot checked over the house through binoculars and said "Something's not right. The main gate is open and there is no sign of anyone, though inside lights are on." He then told Mori to shoot out the main gate camera. If there was anyone there, this would bring them out. Mori screwed the silencer on to his HK33, took aim through the scope and the camera was history. We waited five minutes and then Abbot said "We're going in."

We approached one at a time, Abbot first, then Gonzalez, then

At least Mayhew didn't reveal Duffy's name!
SJ

ABOVE: Rizzo's luxury speedboat photographed off Florida in 2006.
RIGHT: Verrazano-Narrows Bridge

myself and finally Mori. The front door was open. Abbot froze on the threshold and held up his hand. We all assumed he had a gun aimed at him, and next he would drop his gun or be shot, but he turned to us and beckoned us forward. On the floor of the grand entrance hall was one of Rizzo's muscle men, face down, a puddle of blood still seeping into the expensive carpet. He was dead. We began a search of the place, and a few minutes later found the other guy in the study. He'd been garotted.

There were only three ways off the island – by car ferry, by air or by sea. The ferry would entail a wait, as would getting a flight, but Harthaven harbour was only half a mile away.

As we drove on to the harbour, we heard the distinctive growl of a 5-litre marine engine and saw the winking lights of an ocean-going speedboat pass through the harbour entrance. It had to be Picar.

By the time we'd found a vessel powerful enough to catch him and handed over sufficient cash and sureties, we were a good 20 minutes behind. Abbot decided that Gonzalez and Mori should stay behind and liaise with Briscoe – it might be necessary to collaborate with police, coastguard or the FBI, but as a last resort. The onboard radar showed very few vessels operating within a 20-mile radius, which was how far we estimated Picar could have travelled in that time. Only one boat was travelling at over 40 mph. It was headed south. At full throttle it would take us two hours to overhaul him – provided he went no faster. In the swell the boat was launching off wave tops and crashing back with such force I thought it would split apart. But Abbot, who was at the helm, was one determined guy.

After an hour of this, and through binoculars, we could just make out the spume of a boat's hull breaking waves about three miles away. After another 30 minutes we were closing it down and it was within half a mile. The lights of New York were visible on the horizon like a false dawn.

If we could see Picar, he could see us. Sure enough, the increased engine note carried to us on the wind and his boat gained distance.

Abbot had stayed in touch by radio with Briscoe throughout. We entered New York harbour, passing under the Verrazano-Narrows Bridge, gazing at that amazing skyline, forever changed since 9/11 with two of its front teeth knocked out. Abbot said, "We've lost him." Just as we were going to despair, Abbot received a call from his commanding officer.

F.I.R.E. (Forensic Incident Reconstruction Evidence)

REPORT D   REPORT C   REPORT B   REPORT A

Location: Rosemount – Rizzo's summer house on Martha's Vineyard

Date: 03.10.2008

Summary: FIRE illustration showing layout of Rizzo's house and the locations of the bodies of the two men murdered by Picar.

Main kitchen

Entrance hall
Frank Torrey, bodyguard, shot by Picar. Estimated time: 20:55
③

Second lounge

Library/study
Mel Lovett, bodyguard, garoted by Picar. Estimated time: 20:45
②

Library/study
Softshoe locates Rizzo's laptop here and clones hard drive.
①

Incident reconstruction by Van Dyke, R. Abbot

Col. D. Davies
SE/DD33908

05.10.2008

1/2

File note from Col. Davies

I organized the Lear to bring Gonzalez and Mori back from Martha's Vineyard to New York and met them at JFK. There are documents within this file detailing what happened after Abbot and Mayhew commissioned a speedboat to give chase to Rizzo, Picar and our own dear Softshoe. Using Softshoe's radio receiver I left open the channel for the Mont Blanc transmitter Rizzo had purloined from her. I was expecting the worst after hearing the conversation between them at Rosemount. (The signal was routed through Softshoe's cell phone to the receiver in New York).

On the boat journey it was clear that Softshoe now had the pen transmitter in her breast pocket. I heard what she said, but not what the two men were saying. There was too much noise from the wind, engine and crashing water. Softshoe must have hoped I would be listening because she said things like:

"I'm freezing. Do you have something warm I can wear? Thanks. A real gentleman. Are you taking us to New York?"

I'd alerted one of our SE friends, Eric, a Chinese American and superb driver who knew New York inside out. He picked myself, Gonzalez and Mori up at the airport and rushed us downtown. The most likely mooring would be the East Side where it was relatively quiet. But we needed more help from Softshoe.

"Why do your friends in the Mafia want to meet me?"

"I don't know the names Peron, or Gonzalez. Of course I know of Senator Finlay. I'm a journalist, remember?"

"Is that the *Endeavor*?" This told us that they were arriving at, or near, Pier 17.

And then: "I feel privileged, a ritzy, Range Rover Vogue. And black is my favourite colour. I know. I'll shuddup."

When we reached Pier 17 a Range Rover Vogue of Softshoe's description with blacked out windows was pulling away. We fell in a few cars behind and began our tail through Manhattan. On my instructions, Eric made a call to a fellow driver named Manchu who would be ready to collect Mayhew and Abbot at the same pier. Eric told him to have hot food and coffees ready for them. I then called Abbot and brought him up to date.

REPORT A
REPORT B

Softshoe's Journal

Photos of New York from Softshoe's iPhone - from the boat and during the drive through Manhattan.

SJ

Rizzo was the ultimate slimeball. One minute he was infatuated with me, the next he wanted me dead. I'd pestered him to show me his palatial home on Martha's Vineyard for several days. I think he believed that the weekend there would develop into something romantic and he was the type of guy who was not used to being turned down.

Duffy had sent me the RHDC, with great pride I have to say. I followed his instructions to the letter (like a good girl) and set up the device in a closet in the room next to the study where Rizzo had his computer. I knew all this because Rizzo had given me the royal guided tour within minutes of arriving. (Yawn, yawn!) Just as long as the target computer was connected to the internet, the RHDC would sniff it out and go to work.

It was still duplicating his hard drive with all his nasty little secrets when he tossed the Mont Blanc pen transmitter to me. Not perfect timing I admit. Another day and I would have been back in New York with all the evidence SATOC needed. I truly thought he was going to kill me there and then, which may have been preferable to an encounter with Mr Nasty! But when Picar did turn up he had more important business in mind than sticking matchsticks down my fingernails or whatever it was he specialized in. It seemed that he had some 'friends' in New York who urgently wanted to meet with Rizzo and me. Rizzo smelled a big deal and with Peron in jail he was very keen to make new contacts. Rizzo, always happy to show off his toys, suggested we go to New York using his boat. Great! Just what I needed. A cold night in a boat.

Picar said to Rizzo, "OK, you go to dock and get your boat ready. I speak with your lady friend." Rizzo caught the gleam in Picar's eye and smiled at him and then at me in a disgustingly lecherous way. Rizzo drove off to the dock leaving me behind with Picar and Rizzo's two baby minders.

It was only much later that I discovered that Picar had killed the two bodyguards and taken Rizzo's laptop. Picar was made of stone. He said to me on the way to the harbour in a totally emotionless voice: "Later you will tell me and my friends everything whether you want to or not. Unfortunately, we have no time for anything else at the moment." In all this excitement they failed to take the Mont Blanc or my cell phone. Silly boys!

On the boat, Rizzo was like a kid and showed off the speed and luxuriousness of his plaything. That was until he thought he was being followed. Then he pushed the power lever and the boat lurched forward as Rizzo grinned inanely. It was then that I remembered I had the Mont Blanc transmitter pen. I surreptitiously transferred it to fit under the collar of my jacket and became more talkative in the hope it would reveal our whereabouts. Seems it worked.

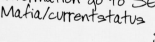

Some background from SE database on the Mafia. For more information go to SE/ Mafia/currentstatus

SJ

article edit this page history

The American Mafia

Also known as the Italian-American Mafia, or Cosa Nostra

search

Go Search

navigation
- Main page
- Contents

toolbox
- What links here
- Related changes
- Upload file
- Special pages
- Printable version
- Permanent link

languages
- العربية
- Беларуская

Description:
The largest organized crime gang in the United States, most active in New York, but operational in most major cities across North America, in cooperation with the Sicilian Mafia and other organized crime groups in Italy.

Origins:
Founded on the east coast of the United States during the late 19th century after waves of Italians emigrated there from Sicily and southern Italy. Began with 'The Black Hand' gang (Il Mano Nera), who specialized in extortion. As the Mafia grew, they expanded into other criminal activities including loan-sharking, robbery, kidnapping, drug and alcohol trafficking, prostitution and murder.

Organization:
The American Mafia is highly structured. It is organized into the 'Five Families of New York': Gambino, Lucchese, Genovese, Bonanno and Colombo. Members rank from non-Italian 'associates' at the bottom, through 'made men' who have been formally accepted into the Mafia by murdering someone either in front of Mafia witnesses or to Mafia orders, usually originating from the Boss at the top of the family. There are strict codes of behaviour and gory corresponding punishments for any breaches.

Famous figures:
- Al Capone (Scarface) 1899–1947 – Chicago Boss in the time of Prohibition
- Charles Luciano (Lucky Luciano) 1897–1962 – New York Boss and founder of the modern American Mafia
- Henry Hill (1943–present) – mafia member whose story was made into the movie *Goodfellas* starring Ray Liotta

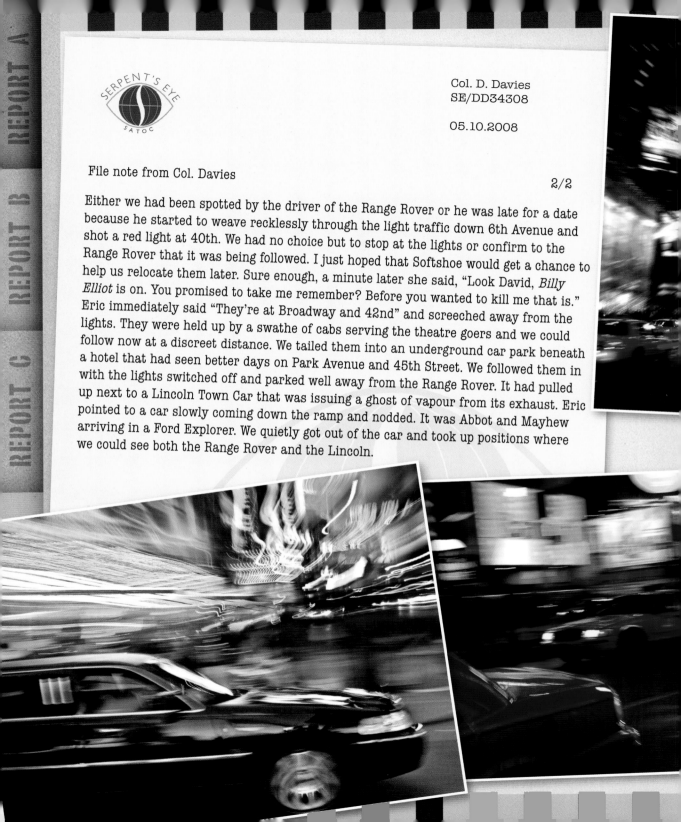

SERPENT'S EYE
SATOC

Col. D. Davies
SE/DD34308

05.10.2008

File note from Col. Davies

Either we had been spotted by the driver of the Range Rover or he was late for a date because he started to weave recklessly through the light traffic down 6th Avenue and shot a red light at 40th. We had no choice but to stop at the lights or confirm to the Range Rover that it was being followed. I just hoped that Softshoe would get a chance to help us relocate them later. Sure enough, a minute later she said, "Look David, *Billy Elliot* is on. You promised to take me remember? Before you wanted to kill me that is." Eric immediately said "They're at Broadway and 42nd" and screeched away from the lights. They were held up by a swathe of cabs serving the theatre goers and we could follow now at a discreet distance. We tailed them into an underground car park beneath a hotel that had seen better days on Park Avenue and 45th Street. We followed them in with the lights switched off and parked well away from the Range Rover. It had pulled up next to a Lincoln Town Car that was issuing a ghost of vapour from its exhaust. Eric pointed to a car slowly coming down the ramp and nodded. It was Abbot and Mayhew arriving in a Ford Explorer. We quietly got out of the car and took up positions where we could see both the Range Rover and the Lincoln.

Range Rover with security modifications

**SATOC INFOBASE
FILE: 385T**

Range Rover has added a fully-armoured Vogue to its range of top-spec luxury vehicles, designed to resist weapon attack from machine guns to hand grenades. Unlike conventional armoured limousines, the Range Rover Vogue Security Vehicle can be driven across all terrains, including urban obstacles such as steep steps. It is the most versatile discreetly armoured vehicle in the world and can be ordered direct from the manufacturer.

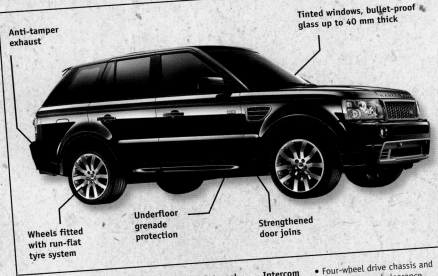

Anti-tamper exhaust

Tinted windows, bullet-proof glass up to 40 mm thick

Wheels fitted with run-flat tyre system

Underfloor grenade protection

Strengthened door joins

Covert emergency lights and a siren available

Fuel cut-off over-ride

Internal oxygen system

Intercom security feature

- Four-wheel drive chassis and off-road ground clearance allows a quick getaway from attack or ambush

- Four levels of security available: the first three offering protection from attack by hand-guns (eg Magnums), assault rifle or high velocity rifle; the ultimate version offers protection to European B6 Plus standard (which includes the Kalashnikov AK47 rifle).

- Up to 2 tonnes of armouring material can be added. The vehicle's body strength allows it to be driven at and through gates and walls. Specially strengthened door joints and handles, so shrapnel cannot penetrate potentially weak points. Added protection to the vehicle's fuel tank and battery.

REPORT E

Col. D. Davies

SE/DD34408

07.10.2008

File note from Col. Davies

Rizzo got out of the Range Rover first, followed by Picar. A window at the rear of the Lincoln slid down. Rizzo said something to someone in the Lincoln. Picar was a statue behind Rizzo. I saw the right side rear door of the Range Rover open very slowly and Softshoe lived up to her name as she flowed gently out of the car and melted into the shadows. I decided this was the moment for us to take them and called out to Picar to drop his weapon. Someone in the Lincoln must have panicked.

There was a double *phtt* and Rizzo fell back against the Range Rover. Picar was already firing into the open window with a gun that had instantly materialized. There was another silenced shot and Picar pirouetted and then slumped to the concrete floor. The rear wheels of the Lincoln billowed smoke and squeals and it shot backwards and, still squealing, shot up the ramp and onto Park Avenue. Within moments it was followed by Abbot and Mayhew in the Ford, driven by Manchu whose white gritted teeth I could see from some distance away.

Lincoln

Range Rover

Location: Underground car park beneath the Park View Hotel on Park Avenue and 56th Street, New York.

Date: 03.10.08

Summary: Confrontation between Picar/Rizzo and Mafia; shooting; pursuit of Mafia suspects.

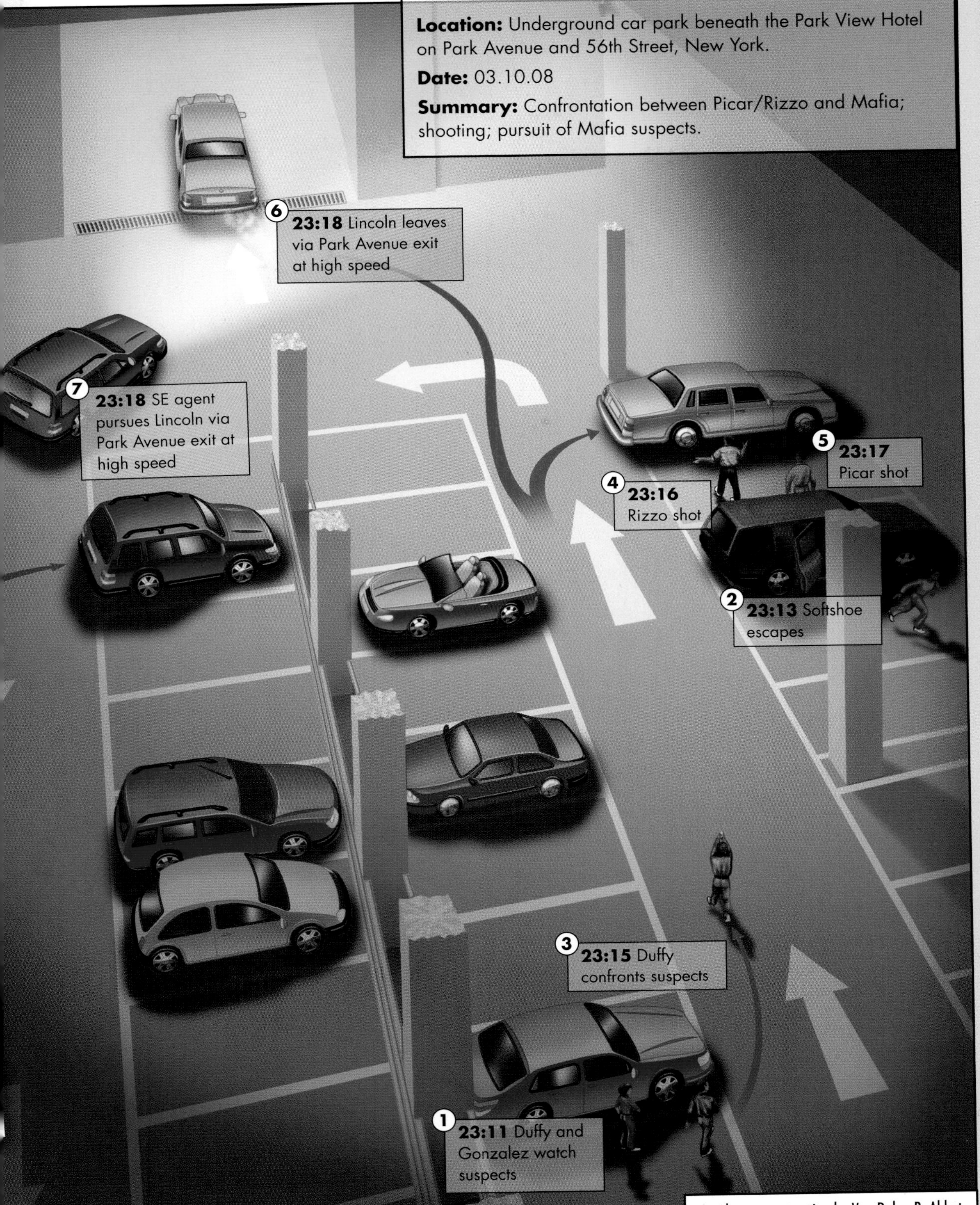

6 **23:18** Lincoln leaves via Park Avenue exit at high speed

7 **23:18** SE agent pursues Lincoln via Park Avenue exit at high speed

5 **23:17** Picar shot

4 **23:16** Rizzo shot

2 **23:13** Softshoe escapes

3 **23:15** Duffy confronts suspects

1 **23:11** Duffy and Gonzalez watch suspects

Incident reconstruction by Van Dyke, R. Abbot

REPORT E

Gonzalez's Journal

We are trained not to take things too personally. I guess I need some more training! It has been hard not to react to Rosco's delight in cruelty, Peron's obscene amounts of drugs money, Rizzo's corruption and greed and Picar's cold-blooded murders. And then the death of a good, kind man in Finlay. I admit it – I got involved emotionally.

But these diaries are supposed to reveal our feelings as well as be objective records of what happened. So here is an admission – when I saw Rizzo and Picar shot I felt a moment of shock, followed by a feeling that justice had been cheated, followed by the realization that the world was a slightly safer and cleaner place. I then felt a hot rush of panic as I saw Rik and Vince drive off in pursuit of the Lincoln. Would this ever stop? I know I had feelings for Rik that were not strictly professional. I'd known that from the moment we trained together months ago. I think Duffy knew too. In that dingy car park that reeked of burnt rubber, gasoline and cordite, Duffy, like the father I'd never known, drew me to him and held me tightly as I sobbed tears of fear, frustration and exhaustion.

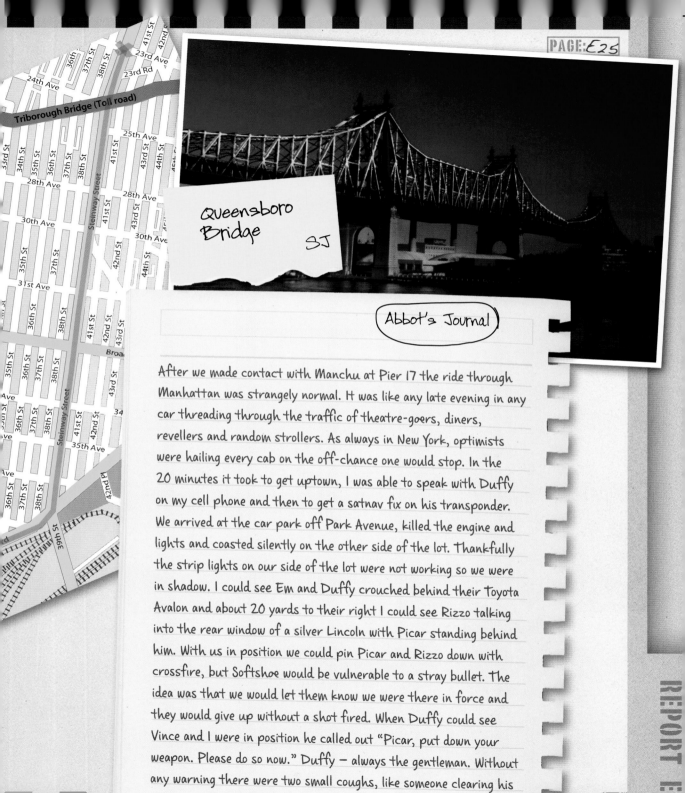

Queensboro
Bridge   SJ

Abbot's Journal

After we made contact with Manchu at Pier 17 the ride through
Manhattan was strangely normal. It was like any late evening in any
car threading through the traffic of theatre-goers, diners,
revellers and random strollers. As always in New York, optimists
were hailing every cab on the off-chance one would stop. In the
20 minutes it took to get uptown, I was able to speak with Duffy
on my cell phone and then to get a satnav fix on his transponder.
We arrived at the car park off Park Avenue, killed the engine and
lights and coasted silently on the other side of the lot. Thankfully
the strip lights on our side of the lot were not working so we were
in shadow. I could see Em and Duffy crouched behind their Toyota
Avalon and about 20 yards to their right I could see Rizzo talking
into the rear window of a silver Lincoln with Picar standing behind
him. With us in position we could pin Picar and Rizzo down with
crossfire, but Softshoe would be vulnerable to a stray bullet. The
idea was that we would let them know we were there in force and
they would give up without a shot fired. When Duffy could see
Vince and I were in position he called out "Picar, put down your
weapon. Please do so now." Duffy — always the gentleman. Without
any warning there were two small coughs, like someone clearing his
throat, and Rizzo fell back against the Range Rover. Picar levelled a

The SE rules of engagement discourage car chases at speed. This is why! SJ

gun and fired twice into the Lincoln's rear window. There was another polite cough from the driver of the Lincoln and Picar spun around and fell to the ground.

The Lincoln burnt rubber in an expertly executed reverse handbrake turn and screeched up the ramp. Within seconds we were in pursuit with Manchu furiously swinging the wheel. We snaked up the ramp and on to East 57th Street and flew across Park Avenue just as the lights changed. The Lincoln was half a dozen cars ahead now. It slewed a wide left arc a block after 2nd Avenue and then scorched along the Queensboro Bridge approach road, straight through the tolls and onto the bridge itself. We kept up by travelling at 92 mph and were now directly behind and matching weave for weave, undertake for overtake. At Queens Plaza, the Lincoln joined Northern Boulevard and then Steinway Street. A figure next to the driver hung a gun out of the window and spat four bullets vaguely in our direction. A shot clanged into the radiator and steam sped past the windows like an enraged ghost. "He's making for La Guardia," Vince said and removed his Glock pistol from a shoulder holster. As we shot past the intersection of Steinway and 23rd Avenue, another shot from the Lincoln hit the windscreen and sprayed us with shards of glass.

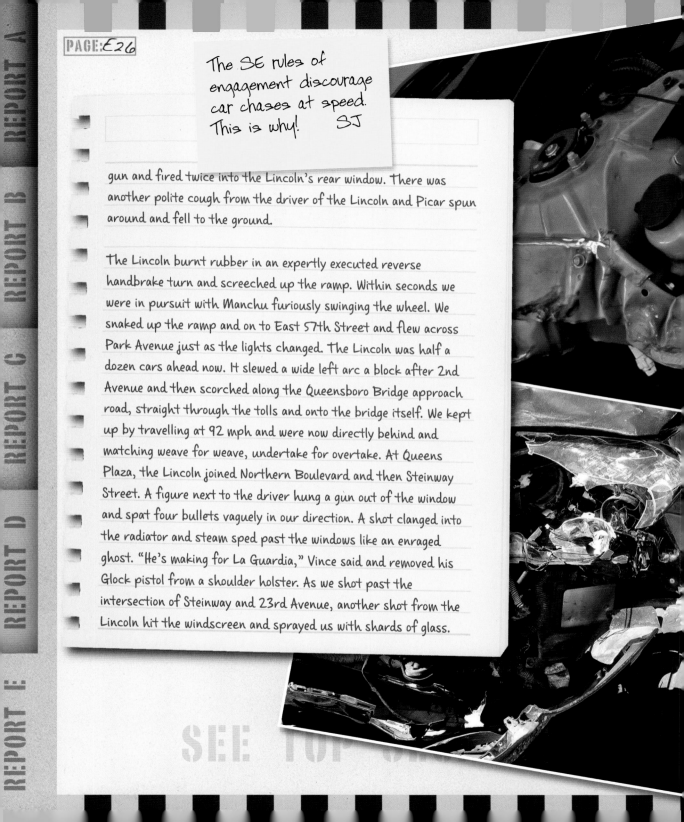

article edit this page history

New York traffic

SERPENT'S EYE
SATOC

search

[Go] [Search]

navigation
- Main page
- Contents

toolbox
- What links here
- Related changes
- Upload file
- Special pages
- Printable version
- Permanent link

languages
- العربية
- Беларуская (тарашкевіца)
- Català
- Česky
- Dansk
- Deutsch
- Español
- Esperanto
- Euskara
- فارسی

According to 2008 figures from the US Department of Transportation, a car crash occurs somewhere in the United States about every eight seconds. A car crash resulting in an injury occurs every 14 minutes, while a car crash resulting in a fatality occurs every 12 minutes. In New York State alone, around 1400 people die due to car crashes each year – that's almost four people killed every day.

Car crashes are particularly prevalent in New York City. Many New Yorkers don't possess their own vehicles as the subway is an excellent underground public transport system; however above ground, around 13,000 yellow taxicabs constantly prowl the city, together with around 4500 limousines and approximately 23,000 service vehicles, not to mention thousands more buses, rental vehicles, privately owned cars, courier and private motorbikes, scooters and bicycles. The pace of the traffic varies from infuriating total gridlock to speeding vehicles that recklessly overtake and take risky shortcuts in an attempt to make up lost time. Around 30% of fatal accidents in New York are caused by speeding cars and trucks striking unmovable or stationary objects like buildings, trees, telephone poles and traffic signals. Nearly 38% of all car accidents occur as a result of cars crashing into other cars.

With a population of nearly eight million people, and renowned for being 'the city that never sleeps', the streets swarm with pedestrians both day and night. Not surprisingly, even more pedestrians are killed in crashes than drivers – often by speeding drivers who hit them while they are on a crossing with the light in their favour. Research has shown that when a car strikes a pedestrian at 20 miles an hour, nine times out of ten, that pedestrian will survive. Raise that speed to 30 miles an hour and the survival rate drops to 50%. In the context of New York's jammed streets, the city's standard speed limit of 30 miles per hour is dangerously high.

Accidents

Vince lowered his side window and took aim as the Lincoln swayed into his sights and fired three quick shots. At least one took out the front tyre, the driver fought with the yawing chassis, but the speed and the spin was too much. The Lincoln flipped into a tumbling roll illuminated by sparks and flying glass, mounted the sidewalk and hit a single-storey brick building boasting a sign that said 'Bailey's Sunbeds'. Further down Steinway there was the sound of police car sirens approaching at speed.

The Lincoln was a mess. So were its occupants. Hit a brick sunbed parlour at 80 mph and you don't walk away. Turned out the guy in the back had been killed by Picar in the car park, the two in the front were Russian Mafia. It looked as though they might survive.

Col. D. Davies
SE/DD52809

21.02.2009

Meeting notes from Col. Davies to video conference of SATOC   1/3

Our avowed aims are to fight terrorism and organized crime, no matter where we find them. With the completion of Operation Lynx we have dealt a serious blow to both.

The loss of life has been high. Senator Nick Finlay's death was a cruel blow to us all, and also to his family, who had not seen him since February 2008. Without the evidence he managed to compile throughout his investigations, this mission would not have even begun, let alone reached a successful conclusion. Eulogio Ruis also died bravely in action. The far-reaching effects of Operation Lynx will stand as a testament to the bravery of these two men.

Juan Picar died instantly when he was shot by Nico Bladic, the driver of the Lincoln. Bladic later died in hospital from injuries he sustained in the car crash. Lev Kuznetsov, consigliere of Russian Mafia boss Viktor Timoshenko, survived the crash. He is now free, for lack of anything to pin on him. Gregory Stutz was found dead in the back seat. The injuries he sustained in the crash were so bad that a post mortem examination could not confirm whether the cause of his death was Picar's bullet or the crash.

David Rizzo was shot twice, both bullets hitting him in the chest. By some miracle, courtesy of the New York hospital system, he survived. He is not fit to stand trial yet, but he will be. No matter what strings he tries to pull, or assassins who may try to stop him, ex-Senator David Rizzo will stand trial. He was being blackmailed by the Russian Mafia. They knew he was well connected with various Italian Mafia bosses. They discovered he was making big payments that Rizzo called loans to one particular Mafia family – the Cordorones. There was and still is a blood feud going on between Viktor Timoshenko and Tony Cordorone. Timoshenko wanted some of the wealth that was streaming Cordorone's way.

In throwing Rizzo's laptop overboard, Picar thought he had destroyed all evidence against himself and Estafan Peron, but he reckoned without the file cloning device that Softshoe had on her keyring. All of Rizzo's files – names, addresses, accounts – they were all there.

Picar had set up a meeting with representatives from the Cordorone family. Picar told Rizzo that a big deal was in the offing, but he was lying. He had told Cordorone that with Peron in jail and the coca plantations destroyed, Rizzo had no more golden eggs to lay. Picar expected to solve several problems at once – get vengeance on Rizzo for being free while his boss languished in a Bogotá jail, get paid for handing over Softshoe to almost certain death, and cement his relationships with the New York Mafia as someone who was looking for a job.

But the meeting with Picar, Rizzo and Softshoe was leaked and Cordorone's greeting party was followed, intercepted and held at gunpoint for an hour by Timoshenko's hoods in a Walmart car park in Queens. Instead of meeting the Italian-New York Mafia, Picar met the New York-Russian Mafia. An unpleasant surprise I don't doubt.

Of the 14 hostages held at the Zaragoza FARC camp, ten survived, including Gonzalez and, albeit briefly, Finlay. Of the FARC guerillas in the camp, six were killed during the Picar raid. Peron set up the attack to implicate the Colombian military, so murdering supporters of his own drugs industry was a price he felt worth paying. Such is the loyalty of these people.

---

article   edit this page   history

The Russian Mafia

Also known as the Red Mob or Bratva (slang for brotherhood)

search

[Go] [Search]

navigation
- Main page
- Contents

toolbox
- What links here
- Related changes
- Upload file
- Special pages
- Printable version
- Permanent link

languages
- العربية
- Беларуская (тарашкевіца)
- Català
- Česky
- Dansk
- Deutsch
- Español
- Esperanto
- Euskara

Description:
A group of diverse organized crime gangs that originated in the former Soviet Union and operate in cooperation with organized crime gangs in Russia.

Origins:
Organized crime has existed in Russia (and formerly the Soviet Union) for centuries. During the 1970s and 80s many Russian mafia members came to the US under the guise of Jews fleeing religious persecution. They established a small immigrant community at Brooklyn Beach, New York, which came to be known as 'Little Odessa'. More organized crime figures arrived due to the economic downturn in Russia after the collapse of the Soviet Union in 1991.

Organization:
The different Russian organized crime gangs have varying levels of organization and sophistication. They range from professional outfits with an identifiable structure, alliance to a leader, and a recognized criminal code, to amateur gangs. Russian mafia gangs in New York specialise in extortion, money laundering, drug trafficking, weapon smuggling, white slavery, counterfeiting and murder.

Famous figures

Vyatcheslav Ivankov, known as Yaponchik or 'Little Japanese', who spent ten years in a Russian prison before bribing his way out and heading to America to become leader of the 'Thieves in Law' Russian mafia in New York. He was convicted in 1997 in a $5.9 million extortion case.

Background info on gunshot wounds. For more go to: SE/ medic/wounds/bullet

article   edit this page   history

Life-threatening shootings

Gunshot wounds, with the exception of shotgun injuries, can appear relatively small and unimpressive. However, bullets are unpredictable and can bounce around the inside of a victim, causing massive and unexpected tissue damage. Three factors need to be taken into consideration to determine their severity: 1) location of the injury, 2) size of the projectile, 3) speed of the projectile. Gunshot wounds to the chest can damage the heart, lungs and major blood vessels. These can be fatal if not treated immediately by providing support to the respiratory and circulatory systems, repairing damaged tissues promptly through surgery, and by taking measures to prevent complications.

A victim of a gunshot wound to the chest will be in severe pain or unconscious, very pale with a rapid heart beat due to blood loss and anxiety, will have an extremely weak pulse, and will be making an awful sucking sound as air is drawn in and out of the chest wound. Fortunately, medical professionals are trained to keep a calm, focused mind to assess injuries, determine whether they are life-threatening or not, and establish the best course of action. Speed is, of course, crucial. To stand the best chance of survival, victims rely on experienced paramedics to arrive on the scene fast – preferably by air-ambulance, so they can be taken to hospital in under ten minutes. Triage methods for gunshot wounds can take as little as 60 seconds. Employing all medical hands and resources speedily on deck to administer treatment is challenging, but not as challenging as facing up to the realization that a gunshot victim is beyond hope.

search

[ ] Go Search

navigation
- Main page
- Contents

toolbox
- What links here
- Related changes
- Upload file
- Special pages
- Printable version
- Permanent link

languages
- العربية
- Беларуская (тарашкевіца)
- Català
- Česky
- Dansk
- Deutsch
- Español
- Esperanto
- Euskara
- فارسی

Width= 501 Level= 203
Stu: 05695
Ser: 001/03   S120   Signa 1.5T   BAPTIST
Ima: 008/015   R   .0 mm   OUTPATIENT CENTR

Rizzo was extremely fortunate to survive. Research has shown that up to 90% of patients with penetrating chest injuries, like his two gunshot wounds, die.

FOV: 24 cm
Thk: 5.0 mm
Imgs: 15/03:59

SERPENT'S EYE
SATOC

Col. D. Davies
SE/DD52809

21.02.2009

Meeting notes from Col. Davies to video conference of SATOC　　　3/3

The body count is far higher than we might have estimated at the outset, but we were dealing with desperate, greedy, violent people to whom the lives of others had little importance. We need to put this figure against the hundreds who die every day from overdosing on drugs traded by people such as Peron and Rizzo, plus the thousands who will die in the future because we have not eliminated this problem, just touched upon it. Then there are the untold number of people, animals and plants that will suffer because their habitat is devastated or removed altogether, not just in Colombia, but wherever the drug traders see farming opportunities. There are the incidents of violent deaths between drug gangs – look at the murder figures in three Colombian towns alone. And then there is that zomboid army of walking dead who do not figure in a statistic of deaths per year, but live in a twilight world of misery and addiction. They steal and cheat to feed their habit before feeding themselves or their children. The drugs don't limit their damage to users, they take whole families.

We have dealt a significant blow to the drugs trade in Colombia and its unofficial US banker, but within two or three years the trade will have bounced right back unless we take more steps of a similar nature. Already we have a mission underway in Afghanistan where there is a tangled knot of drugs, arms dealing, terrorism, bomb manufacturing, insurrection and corruption. As you know, we have information coming through all the time on the situation in the al-Qaeda camp, the changing situation on the Afghanistan/Pakistan border, we have people in place, we have cooperation from the US and British military – all we need is your agreement and everything will be put underway.

Colonel Davies

SERPENT'S EYE

SATOC

SEE TOP SECRET

SERPENT'S EYE

PREVIEW OF THE NEXT OPERATION

SNIPER

CASE TWO:
OPERATION SERVAL

STEPHEN JAMES

OBJECTIVES

1. Assess status of reporter Jules Ivory and soldiers in Wolf 1.

2. Find Ivory's contact. Establish location of dirty bomb factory.

The British patrol that escorted Jules Ivory, returning fire on a Taliban position near Sangin.

SJ

S.E.E. TOP SECRET

SERPENT'S EYE
SATOC

Col. D. Davies

10.02.2009

Note from Duffy regarding a video satphone report from SATOC sleeper Jules Ivory.

SJ

Re: Operation Serval

1/2

Jules Ivory had been reporting for various newspapers from Afghanistan since the battle of Qala-i-Jangi in 2001. Some of her reports, it has to be said, were not instantly popular with Downing Street or The White House, but her courage and even-handedness won her friends in Afghanistan, which is where it mattered. She was recruited by SATOC as a sleeper in 2004 after she witnessed at close hand atrocities inflicted by the Taliban on a village in the southwest. She was a professional enough journalist to know that in a war situation it's never a case of just the good guys against the bad guys, but she had seen wanton violence against women and children that turned her stomach and to some extent her impartiality.

Ivory continued to give her weekly reports to her paper and was once interviewed by the BBC. 'Embedded' with troops while working in Iraq, she managed to go to Helmand Province with the Paras on a few occasions. She sent us reports (see attached) that were so secret and so sensitive we decided not to pass them on to our government partners until we could be sure that they'd been verified.

Her vehicle

Yesterday she sent a report from Helmand by secure satellite phone. See attached. We are trying to establish through Brigade intelligence if the patrol was overrun and if there are any survivors. It does not look good. On the basis of Ivory's report I am instigating a code red for this mission. We will be working in close cooperation with the British and US forces in Afghanistan, but because of the political sensitivities the operation will be totally covert. Since the Mumbai terrorist attack on 29 November last year, the situation on Pakistan's borders has deteriorated. If news of this mission leaked, it could cause the tension between India and Pakistan to reach detonation point.

A photo of Jules Ivory at a press party in London before she left for Afghanistan.

SERPENT'S EYE
SATOC

The term 'dirty bomb' refers to a radiological dispersal device (RDD) - a weapon that combines radioactive material with conventional explosives.
SJ

Col. D. Davies

10.02.2009

Re: Operation Serval

This mission, called Operation Serval, must be given the utmost priority by all involved. If Ivory has indeed uncovered a plot by al-Qaeda to detonate dirty bombs, the global ramifications cannot be underestimated.

And if al-Qaeda had success with a dirty bomb, what would stop them from going further? With abundant expertise and technology on offer from hostile nations such as Iran and North Korea, al-Qaeda's nightmarish ambitions could swiftly become reality.

Colonel Davies

Location of Jules Ivory's last call

Transcript of satphone report from Jules Ivory: 09.02.2008

I am standing a few metres away from a snatch Land Rover on a hillside east of Sangin having crossed the Pakistani border last night at Wanat by foot. This is the first time I have been able to use a satphone. I have heard through reliable sources in Pakistan of a Taliban plot named Kismet to construct a number of nuclear devices. I repeat, a number of nuclear devices. The mastermind behind the plot, I've been told, is Habibullah Haq. The devices will be exploded in major cities, but I don't know which and I don't know when.

The precise site for making these bombs is also unknown, but my sources suspect it is somewhere in this area. They arranged a meet with a local contact, who told me that he will take me to where he thinks the underground bunker is located. (Pause). ▮▮▮▮▮ that was close! Someone is taking shots at me! Ivory starts to run.

Male voice, shouting: Get in! Move! Move!

Sounds of engine revving, breaking glass.

Satphone is showing the footwell of the Land Rover. Voices speaking Pashto.

Satphone is moved and shows faces of three Taliban fighters.

One holds up his RPG launcher and shouts: Allahu Akbar.

One of the others looks for the phone's off button.

(Signal ends.)

Recruitment and training was undertaken by an international board comprising ex-military and ex-secret services personnel as well as experts in logistics and communications.

SJ

/ID: 044523_FO
CLEARANCE: Level 4

NAME:
Omar Mir

aka:
'Gemal Kalim'

SPECIAL SKILLS:
Knowledge of nuclear physics; fluent English, Pashto and Urdu.

EDUCATION:
American school in Islamabad

VITAL STATISTICS
Date of Birth: 17.10.1987
Height: 183 cm
Weight: 82.5 kg

Division: SEE
Base: Middle East

Mir was born in 1987, of Pakistani parents who moved to Kabul in 1980. The Taliban killed his parents, brother and two sisters by indiscriminate rocket fire when he was six in 1992. A friend of his father's had him taken to Pakistan and given an education at the American school in Islamabad. It was there in 2002 that he came to the attention of SATOC – an outstanding pupil with no family and a hatred of terrorism. Under advice from Madi Aziz, the Middle East SATOC sleeper, Mir concentrated his studies on physics, particularly nuclear physics and weapons used by the Taliban. There are other SE operatives in Afghanistan we could use, but Mir's specific knowledge of nuclear physics makes him an obvious choice.

/ID: 0679438_FO
CLEARANCE: Level 5

NAME:
Danny Smyth

aka:
'Piet Stone'

SPECIAL SKILLS:
Wide range of weaponry expertise,
EOD, good Pashto, some Arabic.

EDUCATION:
Army trained (Paras)

VITAL STATISTICS
Date of Birth: 27.09.1984
Height: 180 cm
Weight: 80.5 kg

Division: SEE
Base: London

EOD = Explosive
Ordnance Disposal
(bomb disposal)
                    SJ

Army trained, first selected by SATOC in 2002 when he was 17. An only child
of a single parent, he joined the army at 16 and quickly showed he had
amazing talents and a quick brain. His mother died from emphysema during
his first year in the army, so the army became his only family. In 2004 he
was posted to Iraq in a bomb disposal unit. He learned to speak Pashto while
he was in Iraq, anticipating a posting to Afghanistan.

Emphysema is a chronic
obstructive pulmonary disease
(COPD, as it is otherwise
known, formerly termed a
chronic obstructive lung
disease). It is often caused by
exposure to toxic chemicals,
including long-term exposure to
tobacco smoke.
                    SJ

The Land Rover 'snatch'
vehicles forming Stone's
patrol in Basra.

REPORT A
REPORT B
REPORT C
REPORT D
REPORT E

Col. D. Davies

10.02.2009

Serval – wild cat found in Africa south of the Sahara.

Re: Operation Serval

Attached is a report dated 12.06.2007 from Piet Stone – our Serpent's Eye Operative based in Iraq for a year. I include it as it gives some background apart from the usual profile. I have assigned Stone to Operation Serval with immediate effect. It's vital when reading the attached file to bear in mind some special circumstances regarding the author of the report. Piet Stone is known to the British military through his role in a recent incident in Basra where he was posted as an 'observer'. Stone is one of our most focused and fearless Serpent's Eye Operatives. As the Operatives come of age they are deployed in trouble spots where they use unconventional but effective methods, and if they get into trouble they know they're on their own. We, the military, the government – none of us is accountable. Stone seems to be a bit of an expert at getting into trouble, but he is very skilful at getting out of it.

Colonel Davies

Major Dobbs deploying the remote explosive detection robot.

SJ

Col. D. Davies

10.02.2009

Transcript of incident report from P Stone, Basra, 12th June 2007   1/3

20:50 I was with Major 'Pip' Dobbs' EOD squad in their Blucher Duro belting towards Basra about 30 minutes drive from camp. There was a snatch Land Rover in front and one behind.

IED = Improvised Explosive Device

We'd been on a job to defuse yet another (IED) This one had been placed under a bridge. Dobbs was brilliant – cool as a cucumber when hanging by straps from the bridge girders. We got the device out in one piece and stowed it in the Blucher, which is bad news for the bombers because back at base we'll get to see their horrible little secrets.

On the way back we got radioed about a suspicious-looking Renault abandoned in a street in the west side of Korramshahr. Dobbs felt sure it was a set-up so we used the robot to shoot out the door locks and then approached on foot. He took me with him, said I should lose my IED virginity. He told me to scour the ground around the car for a wire – a bomber might just be lurking somewhere ready to make a connection to a secondary bomb when we were in range. We found no wires, but he was not happy. On the back seat of the Renault was an artillery shell with wires coming out of its nose. It took the next 40 minutes to get to the detonator, the longest 40 minutes of my life. At last Dobbs revealed the circuitry. "My old friend Ali, is it?" he muttered, recognizing the design and the trip mechanism. I looked at his hand as it approached the twisted coloured wires coming from the detonator. "Ali would just love me to cut this white one, but that would be a bad idea, Stone. It'd all end in tears." His hairy hand holding the wire cutter was perfectly steady. The snips approached the blue wire. "This is the one," he said. I could hear my heart pounding in my ears over the sound of the cicadas. The jaws of the cutters closed on the blue wire and went snip. Some time later I remembered to breathe.

As we approached Basra, the stench of raw sewage and burning rubbish filled the Blucher. There were thousands of Shias living in this warren of three-storey white-washed houses, but it was as dark and quiet as a crypt. One klick further on there were a few Arabs around in dishdashas huddled in doorways watching us closely. Others were at tables drinking tea, smoking their shisha pipes and watching us.

Col. D. Davies

10.02.2009

SERPENT'S EYE
SATOC

21:08 A few young Arab men stood in the middle of the road and blocked our path. The snatch vehicle in front of us slowed almost to a halt to allow them to get out of our way. Three Arabs got up from their table and ran into the building behind them. Almost immediately the air pulsed and I felt the jolt of a grenade detonating next to the lead snatch vehicle. Then all hell broke loose and there was AK47 gunfire from every direction. It was clearly a planned ambush. Major Dobbs was wounded in the neck and was unable to give orders so I took command.

There was the boom of an RPG launch about 50 metres to our left. The rocket with its flaming orange tail snaked towards us and exploded two metres short of the Blucher. The blast sent up waves of dust and sparks all around us. There was more machine-gun fire from the rooftops to our right and a whoosh of an RPG over the cab.

I yelled into the radio: "Tango, this is Foxtrot Four, contact wait out!" Seconds later I tried again: "Tango, this is Foxtrot Four...contact at Zero Six...RPGs and small-arms fire...am engaging, over!" There was no reply. I tried again on VHF, HF, satphone and even mobile (recorded at 21:16). No response.

The volume of fire by now was awesome. The cab was being hit by machine-gun fire in a constant *dink-dink-dink-dink*. I feared for the boys in the soft-shelled snatch vehicles, but was also aware that the EOD squad was looking to me for decisions. I could taste fear – metallic and bitter in my mouth. You taste your stomach lining, feel your gut writhe. It's the effect of the adrenalin overload, the body getting ready to run or fight. Some just freeze up.

Fortunately I didn't freeze. I barked orders and our guns spat into action. A man ran towards our vehicle, his Kalashnikov at his hip, firing wildly. I shot him twice. He looked surprised, as though he had just heard some amazing news, and then fell. More RPGs were fired and by a miracle they missed us, but one exploded near the lead snatch.

SERPENT'S EYE
SATOC

The lead Land Rover was badly damaged and I reckoned they were wounded or dead. In the narrow street the lead vehicle would block the rest of us and we'd be sitting ducks. I got out of the Blucher firing at targets as I did so with my automatic and made it safely to the Land Rover. The soldiers inside were badly wounded but alive. I took over the wheel and radio-contacted the EOD to shunt the Land Rover, which it did. We raced away from the scene, but not before another RPG exploded.

(Stone took a sliver of RPG casing in the shoulder. It went deep but missed the heart. Surgeons decided it was too dangerous to remove and left it there. It would cause him problems going through airport scanners, but it could eventually conceal a miniature electronic tracking device.)

Taliban: an Islamist terrorist movement that governed Afghanistan from 1996 to 2001. Since 2004 it has been fighting a guerilla war against the current Afghan government and Nato-led forces.

SJ

Archive photos of defused IEDs including ordnance shells and land mines

SJ

REPORT A

Evening *Times* | Saturday 30th June 2007

Blazing car crashes into airport

A car was driven into the glass doors of the main terminal building at Glasgow Airport and set ablaze.

Eyewitnesses described a Jeep Cherokee being driven at speed towards the building with flames coming out from underneath. It was revealed later that the Jeep was loaded with propane canisters.

Strathclyde Police said two people were arrested and detained in connection with the incident.

The airport was evacuated and all flights suspended following the incident at 15:15 BST.

Prime Minister Gordon Brown has chaired a meeting of Cobra – the emergency committee.

Home Secretary Jacqui Smith said the national terrorism threat level had been raised to its highest level of 'critical', meaning an attack was expected 'imminently'.

On 29 June 2007, in London, England, two car bombs were discovered and disabled before they could be detonated. The first was left in Haymarket and the second was left in Cockspur Street.

SJ

On 30 June 2007 Scotland received its first terrorist attack since the Lockerbie bombing in 1988. One of the terrorists later died of his injuries sustained in the attack and the other was sentenced to 32 years in prison.

SJ

File note from Col. Davies

Since the last file note I have put together a Serpent's Eye team. See profile on Gemal Kalim. Included is a recorded conversation between Kalim and al-Qaeda terrorist Ayman Jafri, which took place in Birmingham, England, soon after the London car bomb incidents in 2007. This was the first time that Kismet was mentioned.